WHATEVER HAPPENED TO
RICK ASTLEY?

Bryony Rheam was born in Kadoma, Zimbabwe in 1974. She is the author of *This September Sun*, which won Best First Book Award in 2010. Her second novel, *All Come to Dust*, was published in 2020 and won the Bulawayo Arts Award for Outstanding Literary Work and the National Arts Merit Award for Outstanding Fiction in Zimbabwe. She has also published short stories in several anthologies. She is a recipient of the Miles Morland Writing scholarship. Bryony Rheam works as an English teacher at Girls' College, Bulawayo and lives in the city with her partner, John, and their two children, Sian and Ellie.

WHATEVER HAPPENED TO RICK ASTLEY?

Bryony Rheam

amaBooks

PARTHIAN

Parthian, Cardigan SA43 1ED
www.parthianbooks.com
amaBooks, Crug Bychan, Cardigan, SA43 1PU
amabooksbyo.blogspot.com
© Bryony Rheam 2023
ISBN: 978-1-914595-14-1
Editor: Carly Holmes
Cover Design: Emily Courdelle
Typeset by Elaine Sharples
Printed by 4edge Limited
Published with the financial support of the Books Council of Wales
British Library Cataloguing in Publication Data
A cataloguing record for this book is available from the British Library.
Printed on FSC accredited paper

For Sian and Ellie

CONTENTS

POTHOLES

When the Bulawayo City Council stopped mending the roads, Gibson Sibanda took it upon himself to fill the potholes along Napier Road with sand and small stones. At first, his job was a thankless one: hardly anyone stopped to say thank you or toss him a couple of coins. In fact, not many motorists seemed to notice that the holes had been filled in at all. They still tore down the road at great speed, oblivious to him standing on the side of the road, shovel in one hand and cap in the other. When they did notice his presence, they hooted loudly or leant out of car windows to tell him to get off the road before he got himself knocked over, 'bloody stupid idiot.'

Unperturbed, Gibson carried on his work, every day shovelling another load of sand into the holes and then beating the pile flat with the back of his shovel. When the rains came, Gibson had his work cut out for him. In the mornings, he would fill in the holes, working hard to make sure that he did not create any unnecessary bumps in the road, flattening the sand with the precision of a baker decorating a cake, trimming the icing here and there, smoothing the top and checking from all angles that no imperfections could be seen. Later, he would watch from the shelter of a tree as the rain washed the sand away, but he felt neither frustration nor anger for there was something he enjoyed about the continuous filling and emptying of holes. He never felt it was a waste of time, but rather that it was part of the gentle rhythm of life, a necessity that underpinned its very fabric.

As the other roads deteriorated, a change took place in the behaviour of the motorists. Some stopped to say thank you to him for his work and give him tips and some even asked him to repair other roads. At first, he was quite overwhelmed with the offer of extra work and moved away from Napier to work on its side roads, some of which were barely strips of tar. However, he soon found he disliked the other roads. They were lonely and badly misused: many of them were beyond repair. The edges of the road were rough, dropping away in sudden gullies that made work difficult.

Then he was beset by a much bigger problem. In his absence from Napier, a gang of young boys moved in and took over his spot. The bigger boys crouched in the bushes whilst the two youngest dirtied themselves with dried clay and stood next to Gibson's neatly filled holes, sticks in hand. As a car approached, they would bend over and pat the holes and then stand back quickly, looking as forlorn as possible, cupped hands outstretched. Initially, Gibson ran up to them, shouting, and they scattered in different directions before regrouping at the top of the road and hurling abuse at him. He picked up a handful of small stones and threw it at them and they ran off laughing. But the next day they were back, and it soon became apparent that he could no longer leave Napier.

One day, early in the morning, Gibson was just walking to his workplace when he noticed a council truck parked up ahead. A gang of workers in blue overalls jumped off and began setting up signs.

'What is this?' Gibson asked them. 'What are you doing?'

'We're fixing the road,' they said. 'Haven't you heard? The vice-president has bought a house round the corner. The road must be fixed so he can travel smoothly to and from his home.'

'But he is never here,' lamented Gibson. 'He lives in Harare.'

One of the men stared at him, long and hard, and then laughed and shook his head.

'There are other roads he could take,' began Gibson, pointing weakly down Nairn, 'in much worse condition.'

'And why would we fix those?' laughed the man. 'This one is not too bad. It shouldn't take us long to finish.'

Gibson watched in horror as the council workers cut a big square around each of his holes and then filled them in with carbon waste from the power station. The man was right; by mid-afternoon they were finished and then they jumped back onto the truck and it clattered away down the road leaving Gibson to survey the damage left behind. The men had made a fire on which to cook isitshwala and boil water for their tea. A hasty clearing that had been made in the grass side of the road was now burnt black. Lumps of cold, hard porridge had been thrown into the bush along with a tin, a couple of torn plastic bags and a scrunched-up piece of newspaper used as a makeshift cloth. Gibson picked up the rubbish and took it to the bin at the end of the road. The bin itself was overflowing with uncollected refuse and Gibson knew that any food would be searched out later that night by the stray dogs of the neighbourhood. Still, he felt the rubbish was in its rightful place and returned to view the rest of the carnage.

He forced himself to look long and hard at the large wounds that had been carved into the soft blue tar. He thought of the gentle circles, how they would no more empty or fill; he thought of the tiny grains of sand and soft small stones, no longer allowed to move and spill, now captured forever, drowning somewhere in the darkness that subsumed them. Bending down, he reached out his hand and gently touched the surface. Perhaps he could remove the black filler; it wasn't tar after all. But the squares would remain, those squares with their hard, straight sides that looked as though they had been cut with the brutality of a backstreet butcher hacking at a carcass.

Anyone walking or driving along Napier Road at that point might be surprised to see a man crouched by the side of the road, smoothing his hand over the newly mended potholes. They might be even more surprised to see him fall forward suddenly and appear to hug the road as his body racked with sobs. But there was no one around for it was the wrong time of day; when the afternoon, tinged with orange heat, is suspended in time, when every attempt at movement seems countered by the force of eternity that reminds us that our lives are only the tiniest and most insignificant of moments.

Suddenly a car shot down the road, a large black car with shaded windows and no number plate. Gibson rolled to the side. His mouth thrust into the sooty black stones; they pressed painfully into his cheeks and the palm of his hands and his kneecaps. He could taste the smell of sun on the road and the thick, oily effluvium of petrol. Dried grass stuck to his hair. The car belonged to the office of the vice-president; they were checking the road for him as a visit was planned for the following year. Gibson watched as it turned off down the Hillside Road.

The visit never happened. Before the end of the year, the old president and his cronies were deposed. The vice-president went on the run and the house remained closed. The road did not last one rainy season and it was not long before the residents of Hillside were once more complaining. By this time, Gibson Sibanda had moved to a different part of town. He went first to Ilanda and then to Famona and finally settled on Pauling Road in Suburbs. There are many potholes to fill in Bulawayo.

THE COLONEL COMES BY

I first saw the colonel as he stood by the pot plants that edged the verandah, looking relaxed in a pair of cream trousers and a white shirt with the top button undone. He was leaning over a large red geranium, a pair of secateurs in hand, snipping off the dead heads with a professional's precision, pushing his hand up through the leaves and searching for any errant heads.

At first, of course, no one believed me. Trish dug her elbow into my ribs and gave me a long meaningful stare with her mouth as flat as a line drawn with a ruler.

'That's not funny,' she said. 'Not funny at all.'

Mom said absently, 'That's nice, my girl. What's he doing? Watering the plants?'

'Deadheading the geraniums,' I said. 'Can't you see?'

No one could, which didn't help.

The next day, he was back for the petunias. He hated it when they got too long and straggly and the stems went brown. He took the seeds off and put them in a small envelope he kept in the top pocket of his shirt.

'You know,' I said to him at last, 'you are going to have to stop this.'

He carried on as though I weren't there.

'This gardening,' I continued, unperturbed. His silences were the worst: you carried on talking and talking and then suddenly he would turn on you and snap. And it was usually quite a bite. 'This gardening has to stop. You need to *do* something. *Say* something. If you want to speak to her, say it. I'll tell her.'

'Rubbish,' he muttered and snipped off the head of a perfectly good purple petunia.

He didn't appear for quite some days after that, and I thought I had scared him away. He never liked talking or discussion. He just gave orders and everyone followed.

One day in late afternoon as Mom and I took our usual walk around the garden, Mom with her teacup and saucer and I with my mug, I saw him just above the lavender. This time, he was looking directly at Mom, and deliberately avoided my gaze.

'He's here again,' I said, glad that Trish was inside doing her homework. 'The colonel. You do believe me, Mom?'

'You miss him, don't you?' she said, softly, her eyes flickering over the large shrubs that grew next to the wall.

'Not that way,' I directed her with a nod of my head. 'He's by the lavender. Just there. See?'

She looked and stared for a full minute before shaking her head. Her teacup shook a little in its saucer.

Exasperated, I turned to him and shrugged my shoulders in dismay. Couldn't he say or do anything, instead of standing there, half-hidden by a great clump of grey lavender?

Mom put a hand on my head and smoothed my hair down.

'Come, let's go inside,' she said.

When I looked back at the colonel, he had gone.

'He wants to tell you something,' I said, suddenly, for although he had gone, I felt it was his wish.

She stopped and waited, as though humouring me.

'He says he's sorry.' That wasn't exactly right, for he hadn't said it, but it was something I felt very strongly as he had crouched by the lavender, the top of his head barely visible.

The cup shivered again in its saucer.

'Whatever for?' asked Mom in a voice like the one she used when we were very young and we showed her the fairy houses we had built.

'I think you know,' I replied, but I was guessing now. I looked round for the colonel to help me, but he wasn't there.

'Bath time,' said Mom.

I stuck a finger in my mug and scooped up the lovely warm sugar at the bottom.

The next day, when we came home from school, there was a man sitting on the verandah with Mom. He had long, floppy brown hair and an unevenly kept beard that looked as though he had attacked it with a pair of nail scissors. He wore blue and purple tie-dye trousers with bottoms that were frayed and dusty from being trodden underfoot and a pair of open brown sandals from which protruded two long, thin big toes, like talons. An unfortunate mark on his trousers in the groin area suggested that he had wet himself, but Mom assured me later that he had not done so. He wore a black T-shirt and two necklaces: one was of small wooden beads and the other was a little longer and a white feather dangled from it. There were beads on a strand of leather wrapped round his wrist, too, and he even had an earring in his left ear.

Trish and I stared at him in horrified fascination.

'This is Mr Patchouli, girls.'

'Ramon, please,' interrupted Mr Patchouli, drawing back

his lips in a hideous attempt at a smile. I agreed. He wasn't someone who suited having a surname.

'Mr Patchouli is here to help me with something very important.'

My mother was never one who settled into nonconformity easily.

She took a sip of tea from her teacup and looked nervously at us over the rim.

Ramon settled back in his chair with the ease of a conqueror. Got her, his stance seemed to say, and there's nothing you can do about it. For indeed it did seem as though Mom had been taken hostage whilst we were at school.

Mom did that thing with her head. Looking straight at us and smiling, she gave a little nod to the left. We could take a hint. We leaned our bikes up against the verandah and went inside.

'There's cheese in the fridge,' Mom called, 'and have as much lettuce as you want.'

When Dad left us, about a year ago now, Mom found it very hard to cope. Although she had trained as a secretary, she had got married before she had completed her qualifications at Miss Tapson's Secretarial and Commercial College and had always been a housewife. Now, she lacked the confidence to go back and finish the course, even though Miss Tapson said she was welcome to. Mom had the fingers of a typist; they were long and thin and elegant. They were also the fingers of a pianist, and she would spend many an hour playing sad, slow symphonies on our old piano. They weren't gardener's hands at all, and it seemed a travesty to see her working outside in the vegetable garden, digging and scooping and ploughing and planting – even though she wore gloves.

My first impression was that Ramon Patchouli was something to do with vegetables or flowers, although he didn't really have the right look about him. He lacked the knowledgeable air and the brisk no-nonsense demeanour of one used to lopping the most beautiful roses off a bush because they needed to be brought to order. Instead, he left Mom with two small stones and a packet of dried herbs.

'What are these?' I asked rolling the stones together in the palm of my hand.

'Now do be careful, Izzie. Don't lose those, will you? They're quite precious.'

'But what *are they*?' I persisted, holding their soft contours up to the light for inspection.

'Well, one's citrine and the other is smoky quartz.'

I waited, expecting further explanation.

'They… they are for something I need.'

'And the herbs? Are you going to plant them?'

'These are dried herbs. No, no I am not going to plant them.'

Any further explanation was impossible to extricate from Mom. Ramon Patchouli's visit seemed to have given her a little boost of life, but at the same time unnerved her. I could tell by the way she played with her crucifix that hung on a chain round her neck. She made herself tea and took it to the far end of the garden where the lavender grew. I thought for a moment she was looking for the colonel and was going to tell her that the last time I had seen him he was in the vegetable patch at the back, tying the plum tomatoes more securely to the stakes.

When she came back, she seemed to have made up her mind about something. It was as though the last hour or so had not happened and we had just got home from school and she was there to greet us.

'Hello, girls!' She placed a hand on each of our heads. 'How are you? How was school?'

She seemed to be her normal self again. Helping with homework, putting the vegetable peelings on to boil for stock and even making a small caraway seed cake. It was only later when she excused herself to do some watering of the vegetables that I saw that cloud descend again. I looked for the colonel, but he wasn't there. It was just like him to run from trouble, emotional trouble that is.

I don't know what made me wake up that night. Perhaps it was just the feeling of someone being outside. I looked out of my bedroom window but couldn't see anything so I put my dressing gown on and moved slowly down the passageway. All the lights were off, but outside there was a full moon and a bright, strong white light flowed in. Mom had moved the small verandah table so it was out in the moonlight and seemed to be arranging something on it. Then she stood back and looked around as though there might be someone watching her – and indeed there was, for the colonel was back to the geraniums and I was behind the curtains in the lounge.

She picked up something from the table and cupped it in her hands, which she then raised up into the air. She seemed to mutter something too whilst looking back over her shoulder down onto the table. It was then I realised she was reading something from a small scrap of paper. She put whatever it was in her hands back on the table and looked round again, like a large cat with its ear twitching. Then she held her hands together as though in prayer, took a reverent step backwards and made to come back inside the house. I darted down the corridor and jumped into bed, pulling the blanket completely over my head. I lay waiting for what seemed an age, before I imagined I had heard her bedroom door close, and I stuck my head out and breathed normally again.

The next day when we came home from school, the house smelt of smoke. We were used to the smell for the colonel had smoked since he was fifteen, although in his later years he had preferred cigars, which had a sweet, dense, masculine aroma. This was different, but I couldn't quite place how. It was a bit like the smell of the grate in the lounge and a little bit like the smell of a bush fire. The colonel used to burn piles of garden waste in the winter, pushing any errant leaves onto the pyre while we would run around adding anything we could find. Afterwards our clothes smelt of smoke and our eyes burnt. But it wasn't quite that smell either.

'What's that smell?' asked Trish, wrinkling up her nose.

'What smell?' asked Mom in a voice a little too wide-eyed innocent.

'Like… like… something's burnt.'

'Like grass,' I suggested.

'Oh, it's just something I was doing earlier.'

'What?' Trish looked up at her suspiciously. 'You weren't burning our things, were you?'

'No, no.' Mom pulled in her lips and shook her head. She took a deep breath. 'This might sound a little strange, but I was burning some herbs.'

'Herbs?' we asked in unison.

'Yes, just some lavender and some sage. A little rosemary.' She twisted her hands and smiled an unsure lop-sided smile. 'I'm... well... I've been clearing some negative energy.' Those last words seemed to roll out of her mouth like heavy stone marbles that fell on the floor between us, scooting off in all directions.

'You see, when you've had a run of bad luck, it... well, it accumulates. It stays with you. And all that happens is that more and more of it comes your way and suddenly you are drowning in it.' She gulped suddenly as though holding back tears.

'What about Jesus?' I asked. Everything about my education had taught me he was the first port of call. 'Can't he help?'

'Ramon says—'

'Oh, Ramon,' Trish and I breathed, heavy with cynical apprehension. His significance in our lives was becoming clearer.

'It's not that Jesus doesn't matter,' she began and then, changing tack said, 'Well, Ramon says they're the same thing. Positive energy.'

We stared at her and she looked back at us, pulling the side of her bottom lip in.

'What about the bank manager?' asked Trish. 'Haven't you been to him before? Couldn't he help?'

'He did help, yes. But things haven't changed. If anything, they've got worse.'

'If he helped once, I'm sure he will help again,' began Trish with sudden enthusiasm as though she had just hit on an idea no one else had thought of.

'It's just that,' Mom interrupted in a halting manner, 'I don't know what to do any more.' Her voice had gone up a pitch and her eyes had filled with tears. I took her hand, which was soft and light, devoid of all resistance. 'There are bills to pay. You two have to go to school and we have to eat. We can't live on butternut soup for the rest of our lives.'

Trish and I looked at each other, our eyes holding the same solution.

'We don't have to go to school,' we chorused in unison.

Mom smiled, a sad, broken smile.

'It's true,' I insisted. 'Trish can help me with my maths and you can help us with English. You can give us titles and we'll write stories for you.'

'Oh girls!' Mom cried, looking down into her hands, her thin body wracked with sobs. 'I wish sometimes the adult world was as easy to navigate as yours. I wish I were a child again.'

'The colonel,' I cried, without thinking. 'The colonel. We have to get the colonel. He'd understand. He always knows what to do.'

'Sssh!' Trish dug me in the ribs with her elbow and did that thing with her mouth that said she would have hit me if she could.

I gave her a look back to suggest I didn't know what all the fuss was about, but I knew I'd overstepped the mark and shrank back, guilty that I had made Mom cry harder.

'What about the bank manager?' Trish hesitated again. Mom squeezed her eyes shut for a couple of seconds and then opened them again.

'I have tried. He said no.'

I couldn't help throwing Trish a look of triumph. Mom and I knew what had to be done. We knew it required more than earthbound things to transform our situation. I held back now but I resolved to try again later to tell her about the colonel. Suddenly I felt more positive than ever.

Another person appeared at our house now on a regular basis. She had a long, angular face with a sharp, pointed chin that reminded me of an axe. Her greying hair was scraped back into a punishing bun at the nape of her neck and secured with an army of large hair grips. She wore long sleeved shirts, however hot it was, and pleated tweed skirts with a large safety pin. In fact, she seemed to be all sharp things, for I noticed she kept a long, thin needle on the underside of her skirt hem.

'Maybe it's for emergencies,' Mom said when I told her, but I couldn't think what emergency might require you to carry that round with you all day. She would also arrive with her darning in a small woven bag. As Mom spoke to her, she'd be looking down at the socks or underwear or whatever it was she was mending, sucking her lips in purposefully, pushing the long, thin needle in and in and out. Sometimes I would get the distinct feeling that she was looking at me. I'd look up and there she would be, staring at me with her grey-blue eyes. Feeling her about to pounce on me, I'd squirm and look away for I was guilty of numerous holes and tears in my clothes. When I looked back, she was still staring, her hands working obediently of their own accord. In, out, in, out.

Mom didn't like us there when she spoke to Mrs Crossack. We could stay for tea and, as Mom always made a tray of ginger biscuits if someone was coming round, we would wait

15

until the plate had been passed round, grab one and then go. But we didn't like leaving Mom on her own, especially as time went on and we had a clearer idea of who Mrs Crossack was.

We would take our biscuits and make a point of saying we were going inside to do our homework. Then we would creep out of the back door, making sure that the screen door did not bang shut, down the steps, and along the side of the house, back onto the verandah. There we would sit, silently munching our biscuits and trying as hard as we could to listen to the conversation. Mom talked about money and Dad and how we had to let the cook boy go and how we'd have to sell the car if things went on the way they did. Mrs Crossack didn't say much. It was as though her lips were full of pins and she couldn't speak in case they all dropped out and fell on the floor.

Once there was nothing, just a silence and Trish and I shared a look and then crept very slowly to the end of the verandah and looked round. My heart was beating fast although I didn't really know what I expected to see. Mrs Crossack standing over Mom's body, dagger in hand? Instead, we saw them sitting close together; Mrs Crossack's hand was over Mom's and they both had their eyes closed. Suddenly, a long, deep man's voice came from Mrs Cossack whose eyes shot open and looked directly at me. I shrank back, my heart pounding against my chest and my palms damp with perspiration, but she didn't appear to have seen me.

There was another lady, too, by the name of Adeline. We were told to call her just that: there was no miss or mrs and, although it seemed strange at first, calling an adult by their first name, and we had to first look to Mom for approval, we not only got used it, it felt quite natural to call her by her first name. She was that sort of person. Not bound by something called conventionality, my mother commented rather wistfully one evening when she had just gone. She wore long skirts in bright colours with tassels and little bells and bits of mirrors embedded in the material. She wore leather sandals that were scuffed on the front and made her toes dusty and a myriad of necklaces in bright pinks and greens and blues.

Sometimes Adeline and Mom would sit cross-legged in the middle of the floor, palms turned upward on each knee, their eyes closed. Whereas Adeline looked as though she had had lots of practice, her smile as sublimely relaxed as a buddha's, Mom was less so. Her face was set into a grimace of concentration and whenever Adeline said it was now time for them to open their eyes again, she always seemed incredibly relieved.

This was called meditation.

'Relax, relax,' Adeline would say, dragging each word out as though it were a hypnosis. 'Try not to think of anything. Focus on now, on this moment. Relax. Reellaaxx.'

It was obvious that Mom wasn't relaxing because she'd fiddle with her fingers, rolling them together as though she had glue on them, and sometimes I'd see her open her eyes ever so slightly, steal a quick look at Adeline and then close them together. It reminded me of praying in church when some of the prayers went on and on and I'd peep out from behind my hands to see what everyone else was doing. I'd usually get a sharp dig in my ribs from Trish in pious admonition. I'd then step on her toes and a scuffle would ensue, ending in us both having to experience the wrath of Mom later on.

'It's your base chakra that's out of alignment,' Adeline pronounced one day. 'I can feel it. It's all about self-worth. If you are out of balance' – here she sucked in a sharp breath of air – 'well, you're on the road to certain destruction. Money problems, business failures, relationship collapses.' Here she looked knowingly at Mom who stared back, her face a paroxysm of guilt.

'Is there anything that can be done?' hesitated Mom in a small voice.

'Well, that's the good part,' smiled Adeline. 'We can realign the chakras. But it will take time and' – here she nodded towards Mom again as though she doubted the possibility this could happen – 'effort. Lots of effort.'

In her stockinged feet, Mom nodded meekly, duly rebuked.

'We need to look at your wardrobe,' said Adeline, casting a doubtful eye over Mom's white blouse and light brown trousers. 'You need to wear more red, more colour.'

'I see,' said Mom looking upwards as though making a mental inventory of her clothes. 'That may be a problem.'

The next day when we came home from school, a figure in red awaited us on the verandah. We didn't recognise Mom at all. Not only did the dress billow outwards as she walked, the two short sleeves lay like a soldier's lapels. It had large red buttons down the front and was made of a fine linen. Mom, who dressed habitually in shades of beige, looked decidedly out of place.

She perched self-consciously on one of the cane verandah chairs while we did our homework, glancing up every once in a while to get a glimpse of our mother so wondrously adorned. After tea, she changed back into beige, tied a large blue apron round her waist and set about making the supper. It was as though she had taken off a pair of glamorous but exceedingly uncomfortable shoes. That night, she lay on my bed, ostensibly to read us a story, and fell asleep. I tried to squeeze in next to her and in the process woke her up.

Jolted awake, she sat up rubbing her eyes and swung her feet off the bed.

'You can stay,' I said for I hadn't wished to wake her. 'I don't mind. There's enough room.'

'No, no, my darling,' she smiled, trying to stretch her eyes open. 'You have a good night's sleep. I have things to do.'

She squeezed my hand and gave me one of those smiles where she compressed her lips and narrowed her eyes as though she had just tasted something very bitter.

'Are you all right, Mom?' I ventured. I wondered if there wasn't something we could do. The washing up, maybe? Or watering the plants. Now the gardener had gone, that was a full-time job on its own. To be honest, the colonel could have been more help, lingering as he did every day by the large geranium pots or out in the flower beds. But pruning was his thing. Watering had never interested him; it was too mundane. Not specific enough and it required very little skill or precision.

'I'm just so tired,' answered Mom. 'So incredibly tired.'

'We can help.'

She smoothed my hair with one hand and smiled again, although this time her lips moved upwards in a curve. Then she leaned forward and a veil of sadness fell across her features once again.

'It's another kind of tiredness. I just can't seem to catch up.'

The next day, there were red roses in a vase on the table, even though we did not grow red roses. The colonel came by, glancing disapprovingly at them. He preferred the small, pink climbing roses that grew along the hedge and the large yellow roses in the main flower bed. Anything he hadn't planted wasn't worth much.

Then Mom hung a long dangly red and gold thing that she told us was a Chinese good luck charm in the front doorway and spent a frantic afternoon going through the linen cupboard in search of anything red. She gave a loud 'aha' when she discovered a red tea cosy and a white tray cloth embroidered with red flowers.

She appeared to be completely in her own world at times, sitting on the verandah with her eyes closed, muttering whatever incantation Ramon had given her for that day or that phase of the moon or to clear this energy or that. Meanwhile, nothing changed. One day, Mom sold her wedding ring. She came home with a purse full of notes that she seemed too reluctant to touch. It sat on the mantelpiece in the lounge for three whole days before Mom eventually put it in her bag.

She was thin; incredibly thin and her cheeks had shrunk inwards like an old lady's. That night we had casserole. She hovered on her chair and watched us eat our food with an odd, hungry fascination while she pushed her small heap around her plate in ever decreasing circles. It became common to find herbs sprinkled in corners of the house and small mounds of coarse salt that were supposed to absorb negative energy. Incense sticks burnt at the table whilst we did homework, the smoke often wafting in my eyes and making them water.

It felt all the time as though we were waiting for something to happen. Every day when we were back from school and threw our bikes down on the ground, we looked expectantly up at the verandah in search of some sort of sign. A sack of gold or a beautifully wrapped present. We wanted someone to appear, their arms around a smiling Mom, and say everything was all right. It was all over, this searching. We could go back to our bikes and our games and our petty arguments and be ourselves; be children once again.

But this was not to be. One day, Mom failed to get out of bed at all. She lay like a small piece of broken porcelain on her pillow and stared blankly at the wall. She tried to smile when she saw us and raised her arm in a weak attempt at a hug, but then closed her eyes and breathed in deeply for the effort was too much.

While the doctor attended her behind closed doors, we sat in the shadows of the verandah step, not saying a word. Pressing my cheek against my kneecap, I drew pictures in the sand with a short stick. I drew a house with a triangular roof and a tree and a flower with large round petals. As time wore on, I resorted to shapes: long, chongololo-like concentric circles that threatened to go on and on, ever widening and expanding.

I looked up at one point to find the colonel next to the geraniums. His face held a look of perturbation as he stared rather dismally at the browning leaves. Of course, watering had gone right out of our minds lately. I expected the vegetable patch looked rather sad as well and resolved to water it later on. He didn't attack them with his usual fastidiousness. Instead, he too appeared to hang back in the shadows as though awaiting some instruction. He did that thing he always

21

did when worried, which was to roll his lips together and then smooth his hand over his mouth, bringing his fingers to a point at his chin.

The next day, a very solemn looking delegation arrived at the house. Mom was propped up in a chair on the verandah, her knees covered in a thick blanket and a shawl around her shoulders. A cup of cold tea sat on the table and Trish was attempting to read to her from a book of inspirational verse we had found on her bedside table. She read in a slow, halting fashion that required her to start the sentence again many times. Listening was a laborious job, like trying to chew through a large, hard toffee. By the time the last stanza was finally ground up and spat out, we had forgotten what the beginning had been.

Trish ended each attempt with a triumphant nod of her head and a knowing smile as though the wisdom of the words was nothing short of life changing. I watched Mom's face closely for any sign of improvement, but her eyes remained closed and her cheeks drawn in, highlighting her beautiful high cheekbones that seemed only lightly covered with a veil of soft white skin.

'You'll like this one,' began Trish after she had studied the next verse with a fierce intent.

Mom raised her hand ever so slightly and coughed.

'I think she's saying she's had enough,' I told Trish, not sparing her any admonishment for I had long ago tired of her tortured, limping verses.

Trish rolled her eyes at me and did that pout with her lips to suggest I had lacked the mental capacity to truly appreciate her words. She stopped anyway and pounced on Mom with the cup of tea. Mom opened her eyes and managed a weak smile and a shake of her head before closing them again. That's when Ramon turned up with Mrs Crossack and Adeline in tow.

They hardly acknowledged Trish and I who were pushed to a corner of the verandah by the sudden inflow of talk of which we were not a part.

Mrs Crossack held Mom's hand and Adeline lit a bunch of herbs and shook the smoke all over Mom: round her head and up and down her body.

'If we could just clear this energy,' she muttered. 'We need to find out where the blockage is.' Here, she looked at Mrs Crossack who gave a solemn nod of her head, looked hard at Mom's hand and then closed her eyes. Ramon and Adeline sat themselves down as though remaining standing could be a dangerous occupation.

Suddenly, Mrs Crossack's head shot up and she stared straight ahead. Her eyes held a startled, glazed look that sent a sharp shiver down my spine. She pointed to the garden as though someone stood there.

'Who is it you need to forgive?'

Mom lifted her head and stared at her for a few seconds before sinking back on the pillow. Her face was damp with sweat.

'It's a man,' carried on Mrs Crossack, fixated on the dianthus bordering the flower bed. Her finger shook like a diviner finding water. 'And his name... his name... is...'

There was a sharp intake of breath from Trish and I as we waited for the pronouncement.

'V,' breathed Mrs Crossack eventually, falling sharply to her side as though the effort were all too much.

'V?' We looked at each other blankly. Who on earth was V?

'Vincent,' Mom breathed weakly. 'Vincent.'

There was a nodding of heads and a general air of accomplishment descended on the three adults.

'Vincent?' I mouthed at Trish who gave an exaggerated shrug of her shoulders in reply.

'Your dad,' whispered Mom, as though she had heard my question. 'It is your dad's first name, but he doesn't use it. It's a family name.' It was the most she had said in a long time and the effort exhausted her. I patted her face with a damp flannel and Trish squeezed her hand. When I looked up again, the colonel was standing by the geraniums.

'Listen,' I said, addressing him directly. 'Can't you do something?'

'We're trying,' replied Ramon who had just lit an incense stick and now grasped Mom's hands in his as though he were going to pull her up for a dance. I looked away. I hated his thick meat slabs of hands and the way the long black hair on his arms crept down to his knuckles like renegade soldiers gone awol from the rest of the troop.

The colonel looked thin and gaunt. Everything about him spoke a kind of grief. He no longer clipped fastidiously at the geraniums or pulled out the weeds in the hanging baskets. The tail of his shirt hung loosely out of the back of his trousers and there were two small half-moons of sweat on his shirt under his armpits. This was the most dishevelled I had ever seen him; I had never seen him so unaware of his sense of self and the result was alarming.

'Do something,' I hissed again. 'Do something!'

A pain shot up through my chest as he shook his head, a

man defeated. I knew then with a sudden and terrible finality that Mom was going to die. I looked round at everything: the verandah with the broken cane chairs, the small table that was really a bedside cabinet, the pots of dianthus and the flowerbeds of lavender and geranium and I could feel it all departing from me in a great rush of air. What would we do without her? How could we live?

She was carried to her bedroom where she lay propped up with pillows. Mrs Crossack sprinkled the bed with what looked like water but smelled like stuffing for roast chicken. Adeline chanted something in a high-pitched voice, occasionally tapping a tambourine for effect and Ramon held her hand with his eyes closed as though in prayer.

Then Ramon looked at his watch and signalled the door to the other two.

'We need to be somewhere else in fifteen minutes,' he said to us, with a smile that suggested his great importance to the world. 'Got a five? Your mother still hasn't paid us for the last visit.'

'Or the clearing,' added Adeline.

Mrs Crossack merely drew her pin cushion mouth in as though to suggest there were many outstanding issues.

Trish got the purse from the cupboard in Mom's room and carefully counted out five one-dollar notes.

'That's quite a fortune you have there,' commented Ramon as he watched her.

'It's our Mom's,' she snapped. 'She sold her wedding ring.'

He nodded and the three left.

It was a relief. Trish and I snuggled beside Mom. I was afraid to go to sleep, afraid I would wake up and find her gone. At some point I must have fallen asleep for I woke up with a start. Mom's eyes were open and she was looking towards the door. I followed her gaze and saw the colonel standing in the doorway. Unsure what to do, he took a few tentative steps towards the bed.

'Dad,' said Mom. 'What are you doing here? I'm not dying, am I? You haven't come to take me away, have you?'

Her voice held an urgency I hadn't heard since she began to decline.

The colonel brought his hand round from behind his back. He was holding a big bunch of geraniums in pinks and reds and he handed them to her as someone might hand over a bottle of wine on arriving at a dinner party.

'Oh, you shouldn't have,' she smiled, laying them on the bed. 'I know how much you love your geraniums.'

There was a pause in which the colonel looked exceedingly embarrassed. His face went quite pink and the words when he did speak, came chokingly out of his mouth.

'This is for you,' he said, handing her a red geranium slip in an awkward, jerky manner. 'You should be able to grow that.' He sat on the edge of the bed like a nervous bird.

Mom took the flower and twirled it slowly between her fingers.

'I doubt I will see it grow,' she said in a voice choked with tears.

The colonel looked away and spoke to the wall.

'I'm not very good at this,' he said. 'Never have been.' He took a big, deep breath. 'I'm sorry,' he said, 'very sorry for everything that happened.'

When she didn't answer, he turned his head slowly to look at her, as though he was afraid of her. 'It's my fault.'

'No, it's not. Of course it's not.'

'I'm afraid it is,' he insisted, taking her hand in his. 'I haven't... I wasn't always the easiest of people, I know.'

'You were a good man.' Her voice was flat, defeated.

He shook his head. 'I taught you fear. To be afraid of life.'

'You were a perfectionist. You wanted the best for me.' A note of irritation belied her words.

'Perfection... isn't always a good thing.'

'I'd say,' Mom exploded suddenly in a strange mix of tears and a bitter laugh. 'Remember how you made me write all my homework out in rough first so you could check it for mistakes before I rewrote it? And remember how you made me make my bed as soon as I stepped out of it in the morning? That was definitely a bit strange.'

He looked away again, by now quite covered in a red that reached his hairline and extended down his neck.

'I meant well,' he began, but she interrupted him.

'Meant well? God, Dad, I'm forty-two years old and I can't bear to leave a teaspoon unwashed by the sink or a cushion out of place on the sofa or... or... put the washing on the line unless I hang the clothes in order of size. I mean, do you know how many *hours* I have spent trying to leave the socks pegged next to a dress and attempting to walk away? Then not being able to. Watching anxiously from the window, all the time thinking that you would not like such... such chaos and having to go back outside and rearrange everything so it is in size order?'

'You *are* angry,' he said. 'Perhaps that's good.'

'There's lots to be angry about. No wonder Mother left.'

By now, the colonel was almost scarlet.

'That was her decision,' he managed to squeak.

'Definitely not mine,' Mom snapped. 'I was left with you.'

The colonel seemed to sink under the weight of her words. 'I'm sorry.'

There was a long period of silence. Mom lay back in her pillows, a tear slowly making its way down her cheek.

'I miss you,' she said at last. 'I miss you, Dad.'

I don't know what happened next except that I woke up again and found Trish's leg boring into my shoulder. I don't know how she ends up where she does. Mom wasn't in the bed and my first reaction was to panic, but then I reminded myself that dead people don't usually get up and walk out of the room.

I found her sitting in the kitchen with a shawl wrapped round her shoulders, sipping a cup of tea. She looked frail still, but there was something that was different, like someone had switched on an inner light.

She smiled when she saw me.

'I saw him,' she said. 'The colonel. You were right.'

I sat at the table and looked closely at her.

'And?'

'Forgiveness is a long process,' said Mom and then she burst into tears and smiled at the same time. 'And there is a lot of it to be done.'

Later that day, we swept out all the salt and the herbs and Mom gave us the crystals to play with. She put the geraniums in water and placed them on the verandah table. I saw the colonel standing by the steps looking in and I beckoned him to come and sit with us. He shook his head.

'Lots to do,' he said. 'Garden's a bloody mess since I'm no longer around.'

Then he smiled and doffed his hat and left us all in peace.

THE PIANO TUNER

Leonard Mwale climbed slowly and heavily down the steps of the minibus, holding the door frame with one hand and beginning to fumble in his trouser pocket with his other. He could feel the impatience of the driver as he pumped the accelerator a little. The conductor waved at him slowly as though he were a child and flashed him a big, cheesy, open-mouthed grin, before looking down at the wad of notes in his hand.

Once out, Leonard wiped his brow with a large white handkerchief and stepped away as the minibus roared off. He let the bag he was carrying on his right shoulder slip to the ground softly. His top lip glistened with sweat as he pushed two fingers into his waistcoat pocket and pulled out a small piece of paper.

He hadn't been to this area of Ndola for a long time. Most of the pianos he tuned these days were at schools, but there were still a few in private households. Sometimes the ladies came to fetch him, or sent a driver. If not, they usually paid his bus fare and gave him lunch. But this madame hadn't mentioned anything of the kind and he was still too polite to mention it. He'd simply written her address down and said that he would be there at ten. He would have to walk quickly if he was going to make it on time. Being October, it was already hot and the tar shimmered before him as he picked up his bag and started down the road.

He was a heavily built man who walked slowly, almost painfully, yet there was rarely a sense of weariness about his person. He always wore a suit, a three-piece in brown. It was a habit he had picked up from Tom Jenkins, the man who had taught him how to tune pianos all those years ago in Lusaka – forty-six to be exact. He remained fervent about it, even when he heard titters of laughter as he toiled along the road, sweating in the African sun, and even when nice madames offered him long, cool glasses of water and suggested he take his jacket off.

When he had almost reached the address of his next job, he stopped for a moment, put down his bag and mopped his head again with his handkerchief. He took his watch out of a pocket and checked the time. He was a minute early. The large green metal gate was closed to him so he pushed the button on the intercom and waited, trying to calm his breathing so he could speak clearly. He needn't have worried for the gate opened and he walked in, up a straight driveway, lined with rows of meticulously trimmed shrubs. To his left was a small patch of equally well-kept grass that didn't look as though it had a blade out of place. On a small verandah were two pots sporting large ferns, and a stack of wrought-iron chairs, chained together with a padlock securing them.

A gardener appeared in the empty garage at the end of the driveway and called something, which Leonard didn't hear, and pointed in the direction of the back door. Leonard opted for the front door, pausing once again to mop his brow before he knocked. A maid appeared almost immediately and Leonard heard the sound of various locks being turned before the door was opened. Despite the heat, the maid looked wonderfully cool in her uniform of dress, apron and *doek*. She had a bright, open face and smiled widely at Leonard, who warmed to her at once.

'Good morning,' he greeted her. 'I am here to tune the piano. Please tell the madame.'

'I know. Follow me.' She stood back so that he could enter. The house, of the old, colonial type, was dark and cool inside. He followed the maid through an inside verandah and along a short passage. She opened a door on the right and ushered him in. It was a sparsely furnished room: a small round table in the middle covered in a white crocheted tablecloth and an upright piano against the far wall. Leonard stood at the door for a couple of seconds, as though awaiting instructions.

'The madame... she is here?' he ventured.

'She will come,' said the maid, but there was something in her voice that suggested it wasn't likely. Leonard approached the piano, put down his bag and pulled out the stool. He turned just as the maid was pulling the door behind her.

'Sister,' he called, and she stopped. 'Some water please. Cold.'

There was that smile again and she closed the door. Leonard turned to the piano and pushed back the lid. When the maid entered some minutes later with a jug of water and a plastic tumbler, Leonard was lost in his work and oblivious to her presence.

When he stopped and poured himself some water, he sat and listened for a few minutes, but he could hear nothing. Then somewhere, far in the distance, he heard a voice calling to someone, probably the gardener shouting to a friend. Otherwise, there was nothing: no television or radio, no sound of voices from within the house, no tread of feet down the passage.

Towards lunchtime, there was a light knock at the door and the maid entered.

'The Bwana is asking if you would like to be having lunch with them.'

Leonard hesitated. It wasn't that he didn't want to accept the invitation; just that he had hoped to get in another job that afternoon.

'Yes, thank you. Tell the Bwana thank you, I will come.'

'This way,' said the maid and pointed back down the corridor they had walked up earlier. Her response took him by surprise and it was only then that he realised he had received an order, not an invitation. He held up his hand for her to wait while he put a few things away, then he pushed the piano stool back into place and followed her.

The maid knocked on one side of a large double door with glass inlay. Leonard heard a sharp 'Come in!' and she pushed the handle down and opened the door for him, without going into the room herself.

A large Indian man sat at the head of the far end of the table, knife and fork in hands, his plate piled high with food. He was in his fifties with thinning black hair and a bulbous face. His shirt collar was open to reveal a thick tuft of hair and a thin line of perspiration was making its way down his face. Next to him sat a tall thin lady with a long gaunt face. Her hair was pulled back into a loose knot high on her head. She played with the food on her half-empty plate with desultory interest. The man looked briefly at Leonard and then took a mouthful of food.

'Yes?' he said, when he had finished swallowing and had wiped his hands on a serviette.

'Leonard Mwale, sir,' said Leonard, extending his hand and walking over to him.

The name obviously didn't register with the man who merely looked at Leonard's hand without taking it.

'The piano tuner,' prompted Leonard with a brief laugh.

'Ah,' said the man. 'And where is the Bwana?'

'The Bwana? I am the Bwana, sir. I work by myself.'

'But it says here "Thomas Jenkins, Piano Tuners",' said the man, picking up a business card at his elbow. 'This isn't your name. This is a *mʒungu* name. Where is the *mʒungu*?'

Leonard laughed; a deep, hearty, good-natured laugh. 'Ah, Bwana Jenkins left this country a long time ago. I have his business now. I am the piano tuner.'

The man didn't share Leonard's sense of humour. 'Mmm,' he muttered uncertainly, turning the card over in his hand. 'The *mʒungu* bwana let you take his business, huh? What, you didn't buy it from him?'

Leonard stopped laughing. There was an accusatory note in the man's voice. He spoke quietly but defiantly. 'He gave it to me. A long time ago now, in 1965. He was leaving the country to go back to England and he gave me his business so that there would still be someone in Zambia who could tune pianos.'

'Hmmm? There is no one else?'

Leonard shook his head. 'Sometimes someone comes from South Africa or Zimbabwe. But they are expensive, very expensive.'

The man appeared to think this over. 'You are good?' he

said, finally. 'You are as good as these people from South Africa and Zimbabwe?'

Leonard lowered his head, a little embarrassed.

'Yes, sir, I am as good as them.' Then he added with a return of his laugh, 'But half the price.'

The man stared at him for a few more seconds before turning to the woman and speaking to her in a language Leonard did not understand. Finally he looked up and pointed his hand to the chair at the other end of the table opposite himself. The maid was called and she moved the mat and cutlery from the right hand side of the man and set a place for Leonard. While placing a glass next to him, the man called something out to her and she disappeared, returning shortly with the plastic tumbler she had brought in to Leonard earlier.

'I have to go to work,' said the man, standing up and pushing his chair back. 'Paying for your piano lessons is keeping me busy at the office,' he said to the tall, thin lady. 'You are going to work me into an early grave.'

She didn't say a word, sipping her water quietly and staring ahead. The man nodded at Leonard and then left. Shortly afterwards, the lady left the room without saying anything.

The job took longer than Leonard thought it would and he still wasn't happy with an 'A' flat, which sounded too dull for his liking. He sat playing for a few minutes. There was some music on top of the piano that he glanced through and chose a light piece by Beethoven.

'You play beautifully,' said a voice from the door. Leonard turned and there was the lady from lunch. He stood and gestured for her to sit down.

'Come, play. See how it sounds now.'

She shook her head.

'I can't... I couldn't... I can't play like you just did. I'm just a beginner. I've only just got the piano.'

Leonard smiled and sat down again. He carried on playing, finishing with an exaggerated flourish. The woman edged nearer, leaning against the table, her arms crossed over her chest.

'Very nice, very nice,' she kept saying. 'Ah, I wish I could play like you.'

'Lessons,' said Leonard, simply. 'You are taking lessons?'

'Do you give them?' she asked with sudden excitement. 'I will pay you very well. Double.'

Leonard laughed. 'No, no, I do not give lessons. I am the piano tuner.'

Leonard accepted payment for the piano tuning, counting it out meticulously. Then he smiled and gave the woman a receipt. She looked at it, reading the name on the stamp.

'Thomas Jenkins, Piano Tuners,' she said and then burst into laughter. 'Thank you, Mr Jenkins!'

Leonard gave her a big, generous smile. He felt sorry for her, as though she were lost, but no one was able to give her directions home.

'Thank you,' he said. 'Give me a call in about six months' time.'

Her face fell. 'So soon? My husband...'

'It's the weather, you know. After the rainy season, it might not sound the same.'

'Okay,' she agreed, uncertainly.

'And I give discounts for good customers,' he smiled. 'Good

afternoon.' He turned and made his way towards the door. She started after him.

'Mr Mwale,' she called. 'My driver can take you home. Let me call him.'

'Thank you,' said Leonard. 'That would be kind of you.'

Later, when he had been dropped at home and had poured himself a glass of water, Leonard removed his jacket and took the money the lady had given him from his pocket. He had not told her it was short. He knew where the money had come from and he understood.

The afternoon is still bright as the electricity clicks off. The sky is still a deep blue and the garden is alive with the softness of butterflies as we make the rounds of flower pots with our watering can. My little girl holds it clumsily over each mass of flowers while I hold the bottom and push it upwards so the water sprays out through the spout. The pink of the daisies contrasts starkly with the soft brown of the garden. At the bottom of the rectangular strip of ragged lawn looms an enormous green-grey cactus, its many flat, round hands frozen in a manic mime of a wave. I collect the debris of tea things and load them on the cane tray: a teapot and a chipped milk jug with a cracked handle; a mug and a child's cup and saucer with a soggy digestive island in a shallow sea of cold tea.

Inside, it is dark. The sun has begun to turn from the house and already there is a coolness in the kitchen, that faint reminder it is winter, however warm the afternoon has been. I grab lightweight jerseys and the house keys and we trot off down the drive to the gate. We have escaped back into the light as we walk down the road. Motes of dust rise and fall in what shafts of sunlight manage to penetrate the jacaranda that line the road and stretch across it, branches touching like a couple in an old-fashioned country dance.

We pass some people on their way home: a man in a weathered suit and a grey hat perched jauntily on his head clatters by on his bicycle with a nod and a smile; a woman walks briskly past, her maid's uniform hanging shapelessly from her, a little too long and a little too big. A gardener with an old, fat Staffordshire terrier ambles slowly along. They make an interesting couple: the man himself is old, too, but he is upright in a dignified manner. The dog is short and squat. Despite the gentle walk, he pants hard and his pink tongue lolls out of his mouth. His owners live in Australia, but he and the gardener live at number seventeen, up the road. Two runners in lycra shorts and vests overtake us, earplugs in, sweat glistening on their faces. They hardly look our way, so intent are they on their run.

We pass a motley of houses: some old, in disrepair, with chickens pecking in the dust and mangy dogs who bark and snarl behind buckled ribbons of barbed wire fences, but run, tail between bony, twisted legs, at even the smallest movement towards them on our part. Old post boxes, paint peeling, lean apathetically in at misshapen gates tied together with electrical wire and torn plastic bags. Occasionally, there are remnants of a name: Utopia, The Range, Pathways. Dusty driveways lead to ramshackle houses whose doors are always bolted shut and at whose windows curtains are irregularly looped.

Rusty metal archways, which once bent under the heaviness of honeysuckle and jasmine, now lean drunkenly across paths that lead to fragments of entertainment areas; cracked paving stones end abruptly yellowed grass and sandy outcrops where nothing grows. The sad, dark windows of the houses look out on empty swimming pools and skeletons of flower beds, the once-ambitious desires of long-gone owners for middle-class respectability. The tennis courts have long been dug up, some optimistically ploughed into vegetable patches where clumps of chomolia are the only signs of green. Ragged squares of asphalt are the only remains of the dreams of the past. A straggle of bauhinias along a fence leans, not so much with the weight of the trees, but with the wait of the years.

One of the houses issues a sign of life. A dog yaps, a child looks shyly round the carcass of a rotting car, a mother shakes nappies from a bucket and pegs them to a collapsing washing line. The verandah of the house is piled high with old furniture and machinery and wound round with a piece of rope – a vague warning to any potential trespassers to keep away.

'That's a witch's house,' whispers Rosie, her finger on her mouth. 'She keeps children and eats them. Ssh! Let's go past *quietly*.' We tiptoe along the dry grass verge, exaggerating our movements and sharing a suppressed giggle. The child watches us, a shy smile on her face, then shrinks back into the shadows. A black car with tinted windows roars down the road and I pull Rosie to my side.

'It's all right,' she says in a matter-of-fact tone of voice. 'If it hits me, I'll just fly away. Fairies can do that, you see. We never die.' The car turns in at the gate of the house and the scrawny dog rushes out, hackles up, barking. The child hangs back in the shadows as a man comes out of the house and kicks the dog. He opens the gate, but the car doesn't go in.

'That's the witch's servant,' Rosie informs me with a knowing glance. 'He's an evil goblin who has to work for her for a thousand years because he once tried to steal her cat.'

An arm stretches out of the window of the car and hands the man a small brown packet then hangs limply over the door.

The man talks, he nods, gives a brief wave and the car reverses, the exhaust booming like a foghorn in the night. Rosie nods as though this confirms some long-held suspicion of hers.

At the corner of the road is our favourite house. Cinderella's house. It is small, but neatly compact. The garden is empty of rusting cars and bedraggled dogs. The low hedge of Christ thorn is always kept trimmed and a small hand-painted sign asks you to please close the gate after you. Not a blade of grass survives the daily sweeping routine, but on the verandah, an oasis blooms. Palms and cacti proliferate from tin cans and plastic yoghurt cartons. Various succulents spill out of old ice cream containers and creep down the side of the verandah wall.

In the middle of it all is a chair and table and this is where we imagine Cinderella sits and purveys her humble surroundings. It is here that she meets with her friends, the squirrel and the mouse, and tells them of her life before she was confined to being a servant. It is here that she sings as she mends her ragged clothes in the evening and it is here, on this very chair, that she will sit while the prince fits the glass slipper on her foot and discovers who she really is.

During the day, Cinderella may be found in front of the house managing a small stall, an upside-down box on which she has placed sweets, single cigarettes, tomatoes and phone cards. She is tall and thin, and today she wears a tight-fitting black top and has wrapped a brightly coloured piece of material around her for a skirt. We stop to survey her wares, Rosie picking up and turning over each sweet.

'The magic ones are red,' she whispers to me. 'Those are the ones that make you fly.'

41

Cinderella smiles. She often joins in Rosie's game. I choose an orange sweet.

'No, no,' says Rosie, her hand on mine. 'Those ones make you freeze.' She stands still, as though playing a game of musical statues. 'Then you can't move for a thousand years.'

'A thousand years?' I say, replacing the sweet on the box.

'Ye-es,' Rosie assures me with a firm nod of her head, as though she cannot believe I have not heard this information before. She looks for confirmation from Cinderella who nods her head at me.

'Well, best to stick to flying,' I say, picking up a red sweet and handing Cinderella a couple of coins.

'Thank you,' Rosie whispers to me as we move away. 'Now she can buy the material for her dress for the ball.'

At the corner of the next road, Rosie slows considerably and her voracious talk dies away to nothing. She looks up at me uncertainly, a finger pressing down her bottom lip, and then across at a dark shape seated next to a fire. The shape does not register our presence. He sits on an old paint tin, huddled over the small flames, poking and prodding them to life. His long hair is matted into thick, twisted coils. All around him is the debris of suburban life: empty tins of baked beans and tuna fish and Woolworths Extra Thick Cream of Asparagus Soup. An empty bottle of conditioner for dull, lifeless hair and a tub of Vaseline. There are boxes and tins and packets and wrappers, each inspected carefully for any remnants that may exist. He talks, but not to us.

'Who's he talking to?' my daughter asks, squeezing my hand.

'No one,' I reply, still in a whisper, as though he will suddenly notice we are there watching him.

'How can you speak to no one?' she wonders suspiciously.

'Maybe they're invisible,' I say, knowing this will rest better with her.

'Yes, maybe,' she says, a hint of excitement in her voice. 'Is he a giant? He looks very big.'

'Yes, I think he is,' I say. 'He's a big, angry giant and he's turned his servant invisible because he was cheeky to him.'

'Or maybe,' she replies, after thinking a couple of moments, 'maybe his servant *wants* to be invisible to teach the giant a lesson.'

I nod in agreement. 'That's right. He stole the giant's invisible spell and the giant is cross because he can't see where his servant is and whenever he thinks he's found him, he moves.'

She giggles and, at that moment, the man turns to rummage through an old hessian bag. Tins clank and something rustles and we jump and carry on our journey. We are approaching new country; even the light is changing. It is a deep green, the green of tranquillity, of assurance, of money. To get there, we need to cross the Magic River.

'Quickly! Over the Magic River! *One, two, pink and blue, magic, magic, keep us safe and true.*' Rosie jumps over a ditch and waits for me to do the same. I take an exaggerated leap. 'Aah, you didn't *say the magic!*' she says despairing at my lack of knowledge of these things. 'All fairies have to say the magic otherwise the goblin will make their boats sink.'

'Their boats?' I ask incredulously as I look down at the ditch laced with empty Chibuku cartons and condom packets. I can quite easily imagine a goblin hiding amongst the rubbish waiting to purloin any unsuspecting wayfarer, but I am a little more sceptical about fairy boats for it is winter and the ditch is dry.

'Yes, the fairies sail their boats from here every evening to go back to Fairyland.'

I go back and invoke her little charm and then jump across the ditch again.

'Don't let the goblin get you,' she squeals. 'I can see his hands and the top of his head!' She grabs my hand. 'Whew! You're okay. I'm so glad.'

We pass the row of houses that have been saved the shame of decline and converted into the regional headquarters of aid organisations. Their gardens have been turned into squares of car park with blue and white striped awnings to protect the shiny vehicles parked beneath. They have signs on the walls with slogans like 'One World, One Future' and a little sentry box in which a security guard sits with a school exercise book in which to record all the comings and goings of all the shiny vehicles. Next to them is a dentist's surgery with a short strip of clipped lawn in front of the wall and the bland perfunctory garden of a business behind it.

Some houses we cannot see; they exist behind walls and electric gates. We hear the tic-tic of their garden sprays and imagine neat lawns of green; flowerbeds overflowing; doors closed against the cold; hot food; the lull of television; warmth. Sometimes we pass huge plots with tennis courts and swimming pools and jungle gyms and swings; where earlier in the afternoon, nannies in smart uniforms sat with toddlers in puddles of sunshine on lush green grass and where now fierce dogs growl and bark behind high fences and closed gates; where notices give warning of alarmed premises and armed response units ready to be deployed. Enormous houses tower above us, like fairy-tale castles with their numerous rooms and roofs and chimneys, reaching up and up and up, competing with the surrounding jacarandas and eucalyptus trees, while fountains of multi-coloured bougainvillea spill over six-foot walls lined with razor wire and through electric fences that zing softly in the dying light.

Outside one, a lawn stretches from the gate to the road's edge – a piece of soft manicured emerald, an unusual sight in drought-riddled Bulawayo. Suddenly, my daughter runs at it with her usual childish gusto.

'I'm a fairy!' she cries, opening her arms wide and flapping them up and down. 'I'm off to the Magic Wood!'

She runs and tumbles, glorying in the smooth green velvet. 'I'm off... off...' she intones, turning round and round. I stand and watch, basking in motherly pride, but aware, too, of the walk home, the gathering darkness. It is then that she grabs my hand and pulls me along with her, and suddenly I am flying, too. We flutter, we jump, we soar and swoop. Across the grass and back, close to the wall and the shut-fast gate and back down to the road.

'I'm a fairy and you're a pixie,' she shouts, commanding the situation. 'Fairies can fly higher than pixies.'

'Ah, but pixies are cleverer than fairies,' I say, as I run up and down the grass verge.

'No, they aren't!' she insists. 'And, anyway, fairies live in flowers and pixies live in toadstools and I think flowers are better.'

'Let's fly home,' I say. 'Let's see if pixies or fairies fly faster.'

And so we are on our way home. The sun slips orange over the horizon as generators whirr into life and electric lights flicker on. Garden sprays are off and gardeners have long ago wound in hosepipes and gone home. Maids have returned to their own children who, heavy with sleep, catch glimpses of their mothers as strange visiting angels before their eyelids close. The old dog and his companion will have reached home a while ago.

Past the Magic Stream with the boats lined up to go to Fairyland and the goblin chuckling with menace as he scuttles off to hide amongst the used sanitary towels and broken glass; past the giant who pokes at his fire and then rocks back and forth, talking all the time to his invisible servant. Past Cinderella who has packed up her stall and returned to her duties inside the house. Past the witch's house where the chickens are now in their coop and the stolen children are in their beds and the dog growls menacingly but without enthusiasm.

By the time we get home, the world is grey with twilight. Our house stands dark and impassive. If we are lucky, the power will be back within the hour; if we aren't, we can hope for it in the morning. I open the door and reach for the candle and matches strategically placed on a shelf round the corner of the door jamb.

The night stretches before us, cold and dark. Rosie is tired now and hungry. She forgets the litany of fairy tales as easily as a piece of litter dropped into the Magic River. I warm milk on the gas ring and cut some sandwiches for supper. By candlelight, we read another story of witches and fairies. We fall into bed, Rosie heavy with sleep, holding my hand tightly against her chest until she drifts off and her grip loosens. I lie awake, imagining that the glimmer of generator-fuelled lights from my neighbour's house are but fairy lights floating in the darkness of the Magic Forest; that our tiny home is a tower that stretches up, up, up into the air, commanding mystery and majesty and wonder in all who pass it by.

I am Rapunzel in my room, letting down my hair every evening, watching it cascade in a blue-black waterfall through the feathery gauze of night, wondering if some handsome prince will make himself known tonight and set out through the forest, sword in hand, slashing through the thorns till he reaches the cold stone wall of my tower and stares up at the dark square of window far above him.

Or I am a princess in a many-turreted castle with a rose-filled garden that stretches all the way to the cliff's edge and a high wall that no one can climb over and fierce dogs that guard the gate. I have children who spend long, hot afternoons tumbling on an emerald green lawn or sailing boats in the pond whilst kept out of harm's way by a host of nannies and maids and gardeners while I dine at banquet tables that overflow with food and wine.

The generator next door switches off for the night and a cold black silence descends. I return to the room alone, folding myself back into my broken dreams. I imagine Cinderella threading her needle and settling down to chat to her animal friends. I envy the Giant his invisible servant and the ancient dog his ancient keeper. But I am happy, for although my tower is tall and dark and lonely, I have not forgotten how to sprout wings and fly. For I have never stopped believing in the magic that will one day pick you up off your feet and let you glide and flutter and swish and swirl and take you off to places you never imagined existed and yet always, always, bring you home safely to the tower at the end of the road.

I settle under the covers and take Rosie's small hand in mine, listening to her soft rhythmic breathing. Satisfied: the darkness is kept at bay.

DIGNUM ET JUSTUM EST

I first met him back in '91. We were both English-language lecturers at the polytechnic in Bulawayo. 'Letcherers!' he used to laugh. 'Courtesy of the British government.'

'Good day, I'm David Hutchins, the new teacher,' I introduced myself on our first meeting.

'Dr Fingall Richmond,' he said to me with a wide grin as he stretched out his hand. His grip was strong, but his hands themselves were rather soft and soapy. I was to find out later that washing his hands was one of his obsessions. He loved to use carbolic soap and kept a great red brick of it next to the sink in his office – he loved having a sink in his office; it made him feel like a doctor, a real doctor. He brought a bar of soap to college every day, neatly wrapped in wax paper and, although I asked on more than one occasion why he didn't leave the soap there permanently, I was never answered with more than a shrug. At times I found it unsettling how many times he washed his hands. I'd pop into his office and find him slowly drying one finger at a time with a hand towel he similarly took home with him every night.

But there on that day of our first meeting, I knew nothing of these little idiosyncrasies. There was always something oddly Dickensian about him as though he belonged to another time with his pocket watch, his two-tone leather brogues and his propensity to smoke expensive cigarillos. The longer I

49

knew him, the more eccentric in his behaviour and dress he became. Despite his Irish roots, he wanted to be the quintessential Englishman. He'd quote Keats in the staffroom and Blake at the bus stop and suddenly the commonplace – a kettle that didn't work or an over-full taxi – was elevated beyond the ordinary and mundane to something more lofty and poetic.

He had missed his calling somewhere along the line and should have been a professor at Oxford teaching Latin or Ancient Greek. I thought it sad at first; an incredible waste of a mind to be sent to some ex-outpost of the Empire, teaching English grammar and punctuation to would-be electricians and hair dressers. I don't know how long it was before I began to see it was partly an act. Of course, I have no doubt he was an exciting teacher; he is the only person I have ever met who could make a lesson on word roots an uproarious affair. I could tell his students came out of class having learnt something. They smiled as they left and took the steps downstairs two at a time. They lacked that look of bored abstraction so common with the young and there was always a cluster of them left at the end of every lesson, asking questions, sharing anecdotes, before peeling slowly away, high on the energy of the lesson.

The girls, of course, were fascinated with him, more than the boys. They stood around him, toying playfully with their long braids, hugging their books to their chests, pushing gum slowly round their mouths. They asked for extra work – extra lessons – while they grinned or winked cheekily at him.

For a while, I, too, was drawn in. I'd find our breaktime talks stimulating, especially after the cultural desert I had escaped in leaving my Cardiff comprehensive where I had spent the last few years battling violent, obnoxious teenagers with little need for anything beyond the rudiments of spelling and basic grammar, if that. I found myself reading authors I hadn't thought of for years, who belonged to the sunny optimism of my undergraduate days: Kafka and Henry James and even a dose of John Stuart Mill.

Occasionally our conversations spilled out into lunchtimes and the odd bar after work. They were always his choice: moderately priced hotel bars that were never very full, with light jazz tinkling gently and waiters with broad smiles. All I had to do was close my eyes and listen. Very easily I could imagine myself in a different age, one of smoking jackets, flannel trousers and spats.

For all his affectation as the perfect Englishman, for all his talk, he kept well clear of anyone white. He abhorred the company of the colonial type with their clipped vowels and standard khaki uniform. The women he detested most, although to my knowledge he had few dealings with them. He considered them uncultured and ignorant, once describing them to me as 'grotesque imbeciles'. In my early days, I didn't question his views too closely. I saw things the way he imagined them and had little reason to disagree. There was, however, one incident when I did doubt the veracity of his remarks.

Our admissions officer was a small, but very sprightly, elderly lady named Mrs Smith. Her white hair curled back from her face in tight waves, the starkness of which accentuated her smooth, powdery face. Blue crescents of eye shadow illuminated her eyes and round suns of red her cheeks. She was a cheerful, smiley person, although she took no nonsense from students. Occasionally as I arrived at work, I would find her opening the office and barking orders at some persistent student. 'Well, you're just going to have to wait, aren't you?' or 'You've no sense of time, have you? I asked you to come and see me weeks ago.'

Once Fingall, entering just behind me, took in the situation with an obvious sneer and darted up the stairs ahead of me.

'Abominable woman!' he remarked to me on more than one occasion. 'Racist. Makes me sick.'

This, in fact, was my sticking point. I didn't think she was racist or abominable. She was a woman doing her job, that's all. I never saw her treat any student differently, black or white. She was efficient, super-efficient, and anyone who wasn't, was duly told so. It seemed to me that Fingall's dislike of Mrs Smith lay more in something else, some other, more real, reason. Having now lived in Africa for many years, I have come to realise how superficial a charge racism can be. It is bandied about carelessly, but hardly ever accurately. The real reasons for prejudice are often more personal.

In retrospect, I wonder if he didn't dislike Mrs Smith because she *was* the real McKoy, a true-blue Englishwoman who knew her grammar and punctuation and her Latin word roots.

Fingall had asked the college typist, the beautiful Miss Moyo, to do some work for him, although I felt his request was superfluous and all he really wanted to do was look down her top and brush up behind her, leaning over her occasionally to point out an error. Mrs Smith watched him knowingly from her desk in the corner, eyebrows arched over her horn-rimmed glasses and her neat red lips pressed together in disapproval. Later, Fingall recalled this disapproval as disgust.

'They can't stand any intermixing, of course. Can't stand it.'

I nodded, but I didn't agree. Not this time. I gleaned more of the truth from a snippet of conversation I overheard one day. We had just come down the stairs into the reception area on our way out to lunch, when Mrs Smith, looking up over her glasses, called out, 'Mr Richmond! The syllabuses you wanted have arrived.' She waved a brown envelope in our direction.

'Syllabi, Mrs Smith. It's syllab*i*,' said Fingall, a perceptible swagger in his voice.

Mrs Smith pursed her lips and handed him the envelope with two hands. 'I think you'll find it's either or,' she smiled. 'Just like hippopotamuses and hippopotami.'

A thick, ugly smile untangled itself on his face. 'I'm an Oxford man, Mrs Smith. I've never heard of syllabuses.'

Her smile spread, too, a thin curve of red. 'I wasn't educated at Oxford, Mr Richmond, but my generation learnt to speak well as a matter of course. We didn't need a degree.' With that, she picked up a large Collins dictionary and turned swiftly to 'S'. Her smile never faltered. Finding the word 'syllabus', she ran her finger underneath it and turned the dictionary round to face him.

'When you're finished, would you mind putting it back on the shelf?'

Fingall was incensed. Red with embarrassment, he strode outside and went off down the road, leaving me to catch up. There was nothing I could say to placate him or cheer him and he would not be distracted. Perhaps this incident explains something of his animosity to Mrs Smith. He hated contradiction or to be shown as lacking in any way. His life abounded in superlatives – he had a golf handicap of 3, although I never saw him play. He had been a top rower, a scholarship student, the best in his year – yet his life as I came to know it was a tattered string of failures that he dragged behind him in ever-decreasing circles.

My own personal confrontation with him came not long after his debacle with Mrs Smith. I even felt there was some small element of retribution in it – for her, not me, but because he feared being shown up again, I took her place. I was, of course, a much weaker character than she was. I hadn't mastered a withering look and quick rejoinders were not my style. I was more likely to retreat like a wounded animal – and Fingall knew it.

Although Fingall taught English language, he always claimed his first love was literature and often his classes would evolve from simple language lessons into poetry recitals.

'Have you heard of Emily Dickinson?' he would ask, eyes closed as he momentarily waited for the expected 'no'. 'Because I could not stop for Death, He kindly stopped for me.' He threw himself headlong into it, his head tilted a little upwards as though he were catching the words out of the air, and the class would listen spellbound to the end. Whether they ever learnt the difference between the present and the conditional future tenses was by the by. They were entertained and he got an inflated sense of his own importance.

My own classes paled in comparison and I always felt as though he was rather scornful of my neatly presented notes and lessons that didn't digress much from my carefully made plans.

'Aims and objectives,' he once read, picking one up and

glancing over it. 'To be able to tell the difference between 'did you' and 'have you'. Exciting stuff, Daffy, old boy. Bound to get them going.'

I could put up with it because, as I have said, it wasn't in my nature to fight back. However, although Fingall claimed his first love was literature, his degree was in History; mine, however, *was* in literature, a fact he never quite acknowledged.

I happened to come into his classroom during a lesson to collect some papers I had left there and heard him telling the story of Venus, whom he mistakenly referred to as the Greek goddess of beauty and love.

'She is the goddess of love, beauty and sexual rapture. Born when Uranus was castrated by his own son, Cronus, who threw the severed genitals into the ocean…'

Immediately, a hand went up. It was a young girl who had recently joined the class. 'Please, sir, I think the one you are talking of is Aphrodite, not Venus.'

Fingall stopped, not used to being challenged in however inoffensive a manner. He was leaning with his hands on one of the front desks and now he drew in his lips and stood up straight.

'And you are?' he asked her, although he knew perfectly well her name was Anna.

'I am Greek,' she said, misunderstanding his question.

Of course, he should have recognised his mistake then and the class would probably have proceeded quite smoothly. However, he insisted on being right and turned to me for assistance.

'Mr Hutchins, would you care to comment? I'm sure you're quite in agreement with me.'

Of course, I would never have shown him up in public if he hadn't put me on the spot like this. I coughed and replied as jocularly as possible. 'I'm afraid you're in the wrong this time, Dr Richmond. Anna's right. Venus is the Roman version.'

Fingall's face tightened perceptibly and he reddened slightly. He seemed to be staring at a spot in the distance. A giggle rippled around the room.

'Thank you, Mr Hutchins,' he said, turning from me and collecting some papers together from where he'd left them on someone's desk. I thought that's where he'd leave it and turned to go.

'Yes, thank you, Mr Hutchins,' he repeated, but this time in an exaggerated Welsh accent. He was grinning now, pleased to have stirred another ripple of laughter. 'All right, Boyo,' he jested. 'Next time I need advice from someone who attended *Swansea Polytechnic*, I'll call you.' The grin was something of a snarl now, a warning I should go. But I felt a flame of anger shoot through me. He had delivered such a low blow, I reeled in astonishment.

'I think you'll find I went to Aberystwyth, Mr Richmond. Aberystwyth University.'

'Ooh, a top *Welsh University*,' he exclaimed, still in that ridiculous accent. 'That's an oxymoron, isn't it? Welsh university.'

He pronounced 'oxymoron' as 'oximeron', an affectation that had annoyed me on many occasions, simply because it was wrong.

'It's oxy*moron*,' I said as calmly and confidently as I could. 'Oxy *moron*.' I turned and left the room, my hands shaking and my face burning.

Although it was a Friday, I didn't wait for him after work

as I usually did. I left as soon as I could and walked through town. It was only four o'clock and the place was humming with activity. I walked to City Hall and bought two huge bunches of carnations. I looked at the wooden carvings, as I always did, deciding what I should take home when I did finally leave. There were some copper wall hangings on sale, too, all with religious verses on them. There was one I liked in particular: 'Art thou weary, art thou languid? Art thou sore distressed? 'Come to Me,' saith One, 'and coming, Be at rest.' It was the exact verse my grandfather had on the wall of his sitting room when I was a child. I leant out to touch it when I heard Fingall's voice from that afternoon. I drew my hand back and walked away.

For the next two weeks, a stony silence existed between us. Not being one to hold grudges, it was me who broke the impasse by suggesting a drink after work. He didn't answer at first and it momentarily occurred to me that he might turn me down. He was marking some work and seemed unusually absorbed in it, his eyes flicking between his mark sheet and the pile of books in front of him. Great flourishes of red covered each page, dominating the untidy scrawls of the apprentice mechanics and the neat round letters of aspiring secretaries.

It occurred to me then that there was something cruel about those long red lines and swirls and the way they looped and crossed. It was more than an affectation, more than a boast. They cut and carved and sliced – and hurt, leaving nothing whole and untouched. But I dismissed my thoughts then, although that impression would remain with me forever and often there were times in the years ahead when I felt myself thinking of it whenever I thought of him.

'Yes,' he said at last. 'In fact, there's someone I would like you to meet.' He said it as though he had some surprise for me, although it was obviously a girl he wanted me to meet so any pleasure would be entirely his. I immediately regretted my attempt at reconciliation for I realised that, not only would there be no apology, I would probably spend the evening like a complete lemon while he toasted and flirted with some beautiful woman. I had been in this situation far too many times and knew how it would end: the two looking provocatively at each other, their conversation centring more and more on themselves and finally excluding me altogether. Eventually, I would get up and leave and they wouldn't even notice I wasn't there anymore.

I decided to stay for one drink. If I left early on, I could at least leave with dignity. As it was, we were there by ourselves for an hour before the 'someone I would like you to meet' turned up, by which time I was on my second drink. When she walked in, it was all I could do not to choke. It was Lucy Ngulube, a student. Of course, I shouldn't really have been surprised. I saw the way he looked at many of the girls, his eyes roaming their bodies, his mouth slightly open so that a sliver of tongue protruded, moistening his lips.

I felt uncomfortable, though, and found myself exaggerating a schoolmasterly tone as though she was there to discuss an essay or ask a question about the use of the past tense. She, in turn, had shed the skin of a seventeen-year-old student and was clad in skin-tight leggings and a boob tube beneath a short black jacket. Her eyelids shimmered blue and long streaks of red shot up the contours of her cheeks.

It was soon apparent from their behaviour that they had

been intimate for a while. Quickly, I knocked back my drink, put the glass down with a determination that suggested, I hoped, confidence, and rose to go.

'Oh, don't go,' cooed Lucy, lowering her eyelids. 'I have a friend coming.'

I smiled as beneficently as possible and insisted I must leave.

'Other plans, Mr Hutchins?' Fingall enquired with a smug smile. 'Not a lonely night in, I hope?'

'No, I'm going out as a matter of fact,' I replied, although it was pretty obvious I wasn't. 'See you on Monday,' I said as I collected my things together and ignored Fingall's lurid wink as I left. Feeling slightly drunk, I walked part of the way back to my flat, wondering if I was an excessive prude; the Welsh have a reputation for being old-fashioned. Yet Fingall had crossed a line and he would never go back. He couldn't and his transgression would cost him his reputation and finally his job.

His students loved him, but as a god, not a man, and they wanted him to be a god always. I was commonplace, ordinary, and, as such, I was expected to spend my free time giving extra tuition or giving away my personal copy of notes because a student had forgotten theirs.

But he was excused all such servitude. He could be selfish, arrogant, dictatorial or downright rude. He could elbow everyone out the way and then tread their dreams beneath his heel, and yet he was still adored for he had acquired the immunity of the gods. That is, until he was pulled roughly to earth.

His relationship with Lucy gave him the proverbial wings

to fly, but not enough to sustain him. After Lucy, it was Priscilla. After Priscilla, Nomsa. After Nomsa, Nonhlanhla and after her a whole string of young girls who, quite honestly, fade into each other until their names are lost and become, in fact, *nameless*, merely a type.

Like Icarus, he soared and, like Icarus, he fell hard and fast towards earth, burnt by the sun of his own ambition. Yet he was oblivious to his fate, exulting in his swift freefall through the air, confident, perhaps, that something would break his doomed journey and he could walk away unscathed. What he didn't realise is a fallen god has no use, for his image is broken. The bright aura that had once surrounded him and blinded him to the limitations of himself faded and died, leaving him in a grey pool of nothingness, alone and ordinary, and there is no one in the world who suited being ordinary less than Fingall did. It sat like some heavy, uncomfortable overcoat that he couldn't shrug off. Like a fool, he clung tightly to that old image of himself, hurling himself into deeper and deeper waters – more and more girls, one-night stands, quick skirmishes in his office at lunchtime and then between lessons – perhaps during them, too.

He was crazy with the idea of himself. If everyone wanted him, it meant he was adored, or so ran his logic. The male students grew angry, although some of them laughed at first. They wrote letters of complaint and stopped coming to class. In the end, he was fired, of course.

I remember his leaving as though it were yesterday. He sat, totally dejected, in his office, staring out of the window at the building opposite. He hadn't shaved for a couple of days and rough black stubble made a shadow on his face. There was another shadow there, too. He looked old, his face rather sunken and grey. Lines had appeared and there was a sweet staleness about him that made me think he had been drinking.

'Where are you going to go?' I eventually managed to ask, trying to keep my voice as neutral as possible. He didn't answer at first and it was only when I snapped my satchel shut that he turned and seemed to see me.

'What was that? Oh, what am I going to do now?' He sat up suddenly and collected some papers together with a burst of energy. 'Well you may ask, Daffy, well you may ask.'

'I've heard there's a job going at Sheriden College,' I volunteered. Sheriden was not as upmarket as we were, but I didn't think beggars could be choosers at this stage.

I saw a little sneer ripple across his face then and his teeth gleamed yellow beneath the curl of his lip.

'Oh, no, Boyo,' he said as he stood up and placed some books in a box. 'When I say I have options, *I have options*. For a long time now I've been thinking of going into theatre. They've been asking me since I arrived, in fact.'

'They…' I thought of the Bulawayo theatre, but then he mentioned some long Ndebele name with lots of clicks, pronouncing it with such theatrical annunciation to suggest he was a native speaker.

'Yes, they've been wanting to get me there for years, but I bore such a faithfulness to this place' – he indicated the inside of his office with a lofty wave of his hand – 'that I felt I couldn't. Now though…' His voice trailed off as he picked up an old hard-backed book of poetry.

'Wilfred, you're coming with me,' he said, running his hand down the spine. '*Dulce et decorum est pro patria mori*,' he quoted, with a smack of his lips. 'One of my best friends,' he said, tapping the book and looking at me for perhaps the first time that day.

I thought him absurdly ridiculous, but didn't say anything, of course, although I moved away and started getting my own things together to leave.

'Oxford men. We stick together.'

I opened my mouth to correct him, for if he was suggesting Owen was an Oxford man, he had got that completely wrong, but closed it again. Perhaps I would tackle him another time, perhaps never.

I didn't see him for a long time after that. I myself got a different job teaching in a private all-girls high school. The money was better, although just marginally, but it was the chance to teach literature again that really swayed me to take it.

I did think of Fingall sometimes, even if with a curious abstraction. I often wondered if he was real. His name, for instance, was that just a fabrication? Some ironic allusion to Oscar Wilde that only those in 'the know' could pick up on? His time at Oxford – was that another story, some snippet, perhaps, of someone else's life? I knew very little of his family; he'd hardly mentioned them. He once alluded to a strict father and an over-protective mother, but another time described his father as a well-read man with strong aesthetic leanings. They were dead, that much I thought I knew, for he told me how he had read Keats at his father's funeral and Tennyson at his mother's.

So much of what we know of someone depends on what they tell us, and they only tell us what they want us to know. It is easy to come to Africa and hang out your dreams. Start your life again, erase your past.

I saw him again about a year after I left the college. I was about to go back to Wales – the first time in four years – to take my new wife to meet my family.

'All right, Boyo?' I heard as I walked along Main Street, hand in hand with Gugulethu. I stopped at once and he shook me firmly by the hand, pumping it up and down with vigour. His hands were still as soft and soapy as they had ever been.

'So I see you like a bit of *chocolate*,' he grinned. 'Welcome to the club.' He eyed Gugu up and down as though he could eat her and she turned uncertainly to me in response.

'Gugu, Fingall Richmond,' I said, a decided firmness in my voice. I deliberately dropped his title of doctor. 'Fingall, my new wife, Gugulethu Hutchins.'

'Wife, eh? How conventional my dear Daffy. Well, mind you, I suppose you were always destined for it.'

His attempt to make it sound as though I had opted out of the joy of limitless experiences fell on deaf ears. Gugu and I were well and truly in love. He wasn't exactly an advert for single life either. Considerably thinner and gaunt of face, his eyes seemed to stand out, giving him a slightly surprised look. The lines on his face were deeper, too, although there was still the air of a learned gentleman about him. It was his hands that remained unchanged – beautiful soft hands with long, delicate fingers that suggested he may play the piano or write beautiful letters in neat copperplate.

He told me he worked at 'a college' and motioned somewhere behind him with his hand.

'Literature this time,' he grinned. 'A bit of the Classics and Latin.'

I stared at him in amazement. 'Latin?'

'Yes, yes,' he gushed. 'All very interesting. A bit of a step up from the poly.'

'Whereabouts is it?' I enquired, resolving to find out more about it later.

Perhaps he caught a hint of scepticism in my voice for I am quite sure that just then a tinge of embarrassment crossed his face, but it was so fleeting that I may have just mistaken it. Again, he waved his hand behind him somewhere and muttered an address that I couldn't quite catch.

'Well, old boy, I must be off. I have the arduous task of listing all the new text books.'

I stood gaping after him and only turned when Gugu put her hand in mine and gave it a squeeze.

'Earth to David! Do you read me?'

'He's mad,' I said as we resumed our walk. 'Mad as a hatter.'

I came later to discover that there was actually an element of truth in his story, as there inevitably was in all of them. He did indeed have a job at a college, but it was a tuition college for 'O' and 'A' levels, much the same job as I had except his students were usually school dropouts doing re-sits or adults studying part time. It appeared that one of the latter was an elderly gentleman who wished to study Latin, which was not offered, and who had engaged Fingall as a private tutor.

Inevitably they fell out as it turned out the gentleman in question said he knew more than Fingall did and objected to being treated as a complete imbecile. I got to know this as the man telephoned my school looking for a replacement tutor. The Head called me in and asked me if I'd be interested. He'd seen I'd studied 'A' Level Latin from my curriculum vitae. However, I declined after hearing the story and putting two and two together. I didn't feel it would have been right, however much I liked or disliked Fingall and however much our paths had diverged in the last few years.

After that incident, I didn't see or hear of him for a very long time. When the trouble in Zimbabwe began, Gugu and I decided to leave. Our eldest child was about to begin school so it seemed an opportune time. We went to London; some part of me recoiled from returning home to Wales, however much I had missed it. It seemed drab and provincial after the deep colour and vivacity of life in Africa. I got a job in a private boys' school and it was to be another six or seven years before we returned to Africa, tired of the persistent rain and gloom.

Going back to a place you have been very happy in is always a challenge. Some places are best left in the past and Bulawayo is one of them. It was like going back into a dream, happy but aware it was not real. Everything was the same; shabbier, of course, and faded, and I wondered how much better it would be if we had returned to find everything bombed to smithereens for there was something eerie and disconcerting about the sense that life had just stopped.

We had kept our house in Bulawayo and, although we had rented it out, our name was still on the gate. Somehow, I expected a letter in the box saying 'Welcome Home' or the beds made and a meal ready on the table. Although I had missed Africa, I found it hard to adjust this time, so used was I to the hustle and bustle of London. I found myself preoccupied with the past, wanting to connect it to the present, but feeling a strange empty limbo instead.

I thought of Fingall then, wondering what may have

become of him and how he had fared through Zimbabwe's dark days. I looked him up in the phone book and asked at the various colleges at which he had worked, but no one seemed to have heard of him. I began to think he may have gone back to the UK after all – or died even. That was always a possibility.

A clue to his existence came one evening at a musical soirée held in aid of an organisation set up to help old-age pensioners. A man had given an introductory speech concerning their plight – their non-existent pensions, lack of government help and the precarious existences some of them led.

During the interval, one of my party began to talk about an elderly man she knew who lived in his servants' quarters, renting out his house to a load of squatters who didn't pay him, but occasionally offered him a few mealies and tomatoes as a peace offering whenever he threatened to throw them out. The house was in a complete state of disrepair and the old man was almost dead from starvation, but now at least the organisation knew where he was and dropped off food parcels once a week.

The conversation moved on to more of the same and then someone mentioned a white man who lived in similar circumstances in a house on Fourth Street.

'Oh, I know who you mean,' a man in a brown corduroy jacket said, swilling the wine in his glass. 'Tall man, very thin with quite a well-to-do English accent? Yes, I've often wondered about him. I've seen him round town a few times. But he's not old – looks rough, but I wouldn't say he's much over fifty.'

'Funny thing about him,' said someone else, 'is that he has the most extraordinary hands. I was standing next to him once in a bread queue back when there was a shortage and he stank to high heaven, but when he handed money over for payment, he had these long, slender white hands. It was almost as though they were the only part of his body he washed.'

It was enough for me. I knew it was Fingall before his hands were even mentioned and the next day found me out on my bicycle, scouring the old part of town for any sign of him. I knew the road, but didn't have a number, although it didn't take me long to find the house as it was an area sparsely populated with white people.

I was directed towards a small house, an ancient, dilapidated building with a square of brown garden at the front and a few straggling ferns in old paint pots on the verandah. In the corner of the garden, chained to the post of what had been a washing line, a fierce dog barked viciously, straining at the collar as he tried to come after me. A couple of chickens squawked and ran out of my way as I mounted the verandah steps to the front door.

A large woman neatly dressed in African print skirt and top answered my knock, opening the door and looking at me suspiciously but without surprise.

'I'm looking for a Mr Richmond,' I said as politely as possible for there was something in her manner that suggested she wouldn't think twice about setting her dog on me.

'He's round the back,' she gestured, beginning to shut the door. As I walked back down the steps, she called to me. 'Are you family?'

'A friend,' I said, turning round.

She opened the door a little more. 'Perhaps you can help him pay the rent. He has not paid for six months now.'

I stood staring, taken aback by the audacity of her request.

'I let him stay because I thought he was a good man. Because he is white, I thought he would pay, but he is a bad man. A very bad man.'

I felt some of the velocity of her words aimed at me, as though by virtue of being both white and male myself, there was some shared responsibility for his actions.

'I haven't seen him for a long time,' I replied, aware that my answer bore no relation to her question, but she appeared to soften, her eyes looking me up and down, no doubt trying to place me in terms of what she knew about Fingall.

'He shouldn't be living like this. It is sinful. *Sinful!* Someone should come and take him away.' Her hand dropped from the handle of the door. 'But maybe now it is too late,' – she pursed her lips – 'too late. Ah, but we shall pray, pray for him to come to God.' With that, she shut the door and I heard a key turn in the lock.

I found him living in what had once been servants' quarters. New servants' quarters had been built further back and looked considerably smarter than his dilapidated squat. He was living in two rooms. One acted as a sort of living room-cum-kitchen; another as a bedroom. Overturned cardboard boxes served as tables and a few meagre possessions were lined up along a plank of wood resting on bricks: a box of cigarettes and a lighter, a bunch of fake flowers in lurid greens and oranges and a small ornamental cat with oriental eyes. For all the poverty of the accommodation, there was obviously an attempt to keep it tidy, if not clean, and I recognised Fingall's presence in the way in which it was kept.

It was dark inside and chilly. Fingall was lying down on a

blanket in the bedroom when I arrived, but he rose slowly, if obviously painfully, onto his side when he saw who it was. He was thrilled to see me, overwhelmed actually. I saw tears glisten in his eyes and looked away discreetly when I heard a choke in his voice and saw him wiping his face with a great dirty handkerchief.

'Daffy, old boy,' he said, his voice laced with forced jollity. 'What brings you to these parts?'

'I've been away. We were away for some years, but now we're back and I thought I'd look you up and see how you were.'

'You looked me up?' He broke into an ironic laugh and holding up his hand he turned a circle in the room. 'This place is in the phone book?'

'Well, not quite,' I smiled. 'It's a long story. Let's just say your reputation precedes you.'

He raised his eyebrows and gave another short laugh. Then he felt in the pockets of the old grey Bermuda shorts he was wearing and bought out a box of cigarettes. It was empty so he tossed it out of the door and reached over for the one on the makeshift shelf. He offered me the box, shrugged when I declined, and lit a cigarette, his hands shaking profusely.

It was hard to know where to start a conversation and for what seemed a long time we just sat, me taking in the sparse poverty of his life and he smoking quietly. He had a beard now, not very long, but not particularly well kept. It was speckled with grey as was his hair and eyebrows. The lines on his face were deeper and his whole being seemed older and prematurely so. He was very thin; I could see his rib cage through the threadbare T-shirt he had on.

I told him what I'd been doing and he nodded every now and then and blew out thin plumes of smoke.

'Well, you've been quite the success story,' he said, but there was no tinge of irony in his voice. In fact, he seemed almost proud of me, as though I were a son of his that he could pat on the back and congratulate. 'I taught you well, didn't I?'

'What do you mean?' I asked. He still had the capacity to rile me, all these years on.

'Well, it was me who persuaded you to leave the college, wasn't it? If I hadn't, you'd still be there now, teaching morons the difference between the definite and indefinite article.'

'I don't remember you persuading me of anything of the kind,' I said, quietly.

He stared hard at me for half a minute and then shrugged. 'Yes, you're probably right, Boyo. You're probably right.'

There was a silence between us and I found myself suddenly so incredibly sad; tears filled my eyes. I fought against them by lashing out in anger.

'How the hell did it come to this, Fingall?' I indicated the room with my upturned hands.

He didn't answer at first, one hand searching in his pocket for his cigarette box. He found it and lit another cigarette.

'I don't usually chain smoke,' he coughed, indicating the cigarette. 'But then I don't usually get many visitors.' He had another fit of coughing before he answered. 'I made a few bad decisions.' He shrugged. 'Happens to us all, I suppose.'

That afternoon he was the most lucid I had ever known him. He told me of his addiction to alcohol and women; how he lost one job after another and finally ended up where he was. He knew his time left was short. 'I have to pay the price,' he said to me with a humourless laugh. 'You can't live the way I have and not pay for it. Dignum et justum est, Daffy, old boy. Dignum et justum est.'

I left him that day feeling rather sad, but content, too, that I had found him and that, if it was any consolation at all, he had one friend in this big, lonely world. It was too late to start the drugs that might have prolonged his life. I paid his rent and bought him food, but he wasn't much interested in anything beyond porridge. I bought some reed mats and each time I visited I would drag him outside so that he could lie in the sun. I offered to read to him, but he waved my suggestion away weakly. He had already gone beyond the comforts of this world.

He died one day in the winter and his body was cremated the next week. I thought of somewhere suitable to sprinkle his ashes, but it was a hard one as he was very much an urban man. I thought of burying them in my garden and planting a rose bush on top, but there was something far too domesticated about the idea. Besides, I didn't want him as close as that. He needed to be set free, to wander the earth without fear of restraint. In the end, I took the ashes to Hillside Dams and sprinkled them on the water. Some flew out onto the air and were carried away in the wind. I took his book of poetry with me and let it open where it fell naturally. I had nothing planned but thought this attempt at a secular bibliomancy would please him.

Move him into the sun —
Gently its touch awoke him once

71

I turned to the front of the book where there was an inscription: *To our dearest Fynn, on the occasion of your 18th Birthday. Love Mother and Father.*

There had been a time when I'd seriously thought of investigating the details of Fingall's life: contacting Oxford or writing to his parents if I could find an address – just to see if they were alive, to see if any of his life had been true. But now I shut the book and resolved to leave him where he was. I walked away, pulling my jacket closer to me, the weak winter sun welcome in the cool wind. I had forgotten how cold Bulawayo could be.

THE BIG TRIP

Mary Phiri slowly pulled on a pair of rubber gloves, squirted some washing-up liquid into the sink full of hot water, and prepared to wash up the breakfast dishes. She watched the bubbles froth before she picked up a cloth and swirled it round the first bowl. The remnants of cornflakes and milk floated into the clear water. She then put the clean bowl into another sink of clean water and rinsed off the excess soap. She always felt a twinge of guilt about the second sink, although she reasoned with herself that after all this was England where there was plenty of water. No need to worry.

It was something her father-in-law would comment on. '*Aish!* Such waste! In Bulawayo, we'd have all bathed and done a week's washing in that. Hey, Fadzai?'

Fadzai was her mother-in-law. She'd watch everything that Mary did with a strange sort of fascination. 'Ah, ah, ah,' she'd gasp as Mary used the washing machine for small loads of whites: a T-shirt, a pair of socks and a pillowcase. Once, she'd almost rugby-tackled Mary at the dustbin when she was about to throw away some out-of-date eggs; and her daughter-in-law knew she came into the kitchen at night and took reusable containers such as ice-cream cartons and juice bottles out of the bin, washed them and hoarded them in her room. What she did with them, Mary never really knew. Took them back to Zimbabwe, she supposed, and gave them to all her friends.

'*She* was going to *throw* these away! Ah, such waste, such waste.' Mary imagined the customs officials at Harare airport opening Fadzai's case and finding, not electronic goods, cheap make up or clothes for resale, but plastic containers, hundreds of them, and Fadzai explaining with similar indignation. '*My daughter-in-law! She* was going to *throw these away!*'

Mary heaved a deep sigh and looked out of the window onto a warm, hazy mid-summer morning in London. Two days, that's all, she thought. Two days and they'll be here again. 'Why?' she'd asked Sam. 'Why do they have to come so soon?' They'd only been last year and then they'd stayed almost two months. *Two months!* 'They're my parents,' he said, as if that answered everything. What he meant was that he wanted them to see how well he'd done. He knew that meant a lot to them. Their son. Something to talk about back home.

They didn't include her in this success. She was Sam's wife. Full stop. Not their choice, but if Sam was happy… And yet wasn't it she who ferried them from shopping mall to shopping mall, who had to endure their presence at the supermarket as they oohed and aahed over the variety of toilet rolls available and choice of bread? 'Not just Lobels Super White, heh?' Leonard would guffaw loudly every time they went into Tesco. She had once found him at the cheese counter pointing a fat finger at the glass. 'What's *that*?' he was asking the assistant, a mixture of fascination and distaste in his voice. 'Cheddar with cranberries,' answered the assistant brightly, 'and that's Emmental and Jaalsberg…'

'Wait, wait, wait,' said Leonard, holding up his hand. 'Yarl what?'

'Jaalsberg.'

'Looks like big holes to me. Hey, Mary, look, this man wants to sell me cheese that's been eaten by some big rat!' He laughed loudly and for too long. The assistant smiled weakly and moved off to serve someone else. Mary rolled her eyes.

It was the same when they went to restaurants.

'*How* much for a starter?' Leonard would blast at the top of his voice. Fadzai would laugh loudly too. '*Aish*, I bought my house in Hillside for less than that!'

'Dad, it's OK, we're paying,' Sam would insist and Mary, inwardly, would agree: 'We certainly are.'

'I'd like some sadza,' Leonard once announced in his customary brash voice to a waiter at an Italian restaurant. The waiter looked over Leonard's shoulder at the menu, trying hard to find which dish Leonard was referring to. Sam laughed to please his father and then smiled good-naturedly at the waiter and ordered a lasagne.

'No, no. I said I wanted sadza,' Leonard insisted. 'Sa-dza. You got that here?'

The waiter shook his head apologetically.

'You come to my country and I'll show you real food. OK?'

The waiter nodded.

'OK.'

When he'd gone, Leonard leaned over the table to Sam and whispered loudly: 'How come they've got white waiters here, heh?'

'And white people working in shops,' chipped in Fadzai, 'and I even saw a white person sweeping in the street.'

'This is England,' said Mary, and Leonard had leaned back in his seat and exchanged a glance with his wife as if to say that was no excuse at all and they didn't quite believe her anyway.

On their last visit, Mary had met them at the airport as Sam was away in Geneva. *Our son in Geneva!* They had to get a train into London, but the ticket office was closed and Leonard had stood outside, shouting as usual, about the time of day that things started to happen in the UK. 'In Zimbabwe, I would've been at work for two and a half hours now,' he had told a man in the queue, 'and this guy,' – he had nodded to the man opening the ticket counter – 'has only just come in.'

'That's not the problem…' Mary had started to say, but gave up. They would never believe her.

***

Mary and Sam had lived in the UK for four years. Four long years. Mary didn't think of Zimbabwe as her home anymore. Her parents had died and she didn't have the long extended family that Sam possessed and so felt little need to keep up to date with events there. Sure, she'd heard about food shortages, electricity cuts and the non-availability of fuel, but when she watched the clips of Zimbabwe that sometimes appeared on the BBC or ITV, she felt she may as well be watching events in Guatemala or Ukraine, places she had not only never been to, but had no intention of visiting either.

Zimbabweans were moaners. They moaned about this and they moaned about that and they didn't know how good they had it. Sam worked until eight o'clock at night sometimes; they had a mortgage that would take them twenty-five years to pay off and it was only a small semi-detached house that they'd bought. What did Zimbabweans know about road tax,

M.O.T.s, council tax, queues on the M25 to work, traffic jams, the cost of living? They saw only fifteen different types of bread and expensive cheese with holes in it. Two-for-one offers on ice cream and eat-as-much-as-you-like pizza. They didn't have a clue.

The week after Leonard and Fadzai had arrived on their last visit, Sam had asked their neighbours round to meet his parents. Mike and Glenda Robson from next door. A white couple. Always friendly, always interested, although Mary never wanted to indulge in their 'So you're from Zimbabwe' talk. Mary removed herself to the kitchen to put the finishing touches to some snacks she'd prepared earlier. When she re-entered the living room, Leonard was busy telling Mike about the size of his garden.

'You see this street,' he said, beer in hand, pointing towards the door. 'You see this street *and* the other one, that's the size of my back garden.'

Mike's eyes rolled in awe.

'Really?' said Glenda to Fadzai and Fadzai nodded her head in affirmation. 'I always thought, well we always thought, that well, you were all quite, well, poor... the TV...'

'You should see a *rich* man's house!' burst in Leonard, almost foaming at the mouth with pride.

'So you mean, what you see on the telly isn't true? I mean, what about Robert Mugabe, what do you feel about him?'

Leonard waved his president away with his hand. 'Who cares?'

***

The night before his parents were due to arrive, Sam told Mary that he had put in an application for his parents to move to the UK. Mary froze.

'*What?*' she couldn't help bursting out.

Sam touched her shoulder lightly. 'Come on, Mary, things are hard for them. Zim is a tough place these days.'

Mary didn't speak to Sam again. They drove in silence to Gatwick and found their way to the arrivals hall. The plane was delayed. Mary could almost hear Leonard's rendition of their trip, how he had to ask for five Mazoe oranges as that would be the last time he would be drinking proper orange juice for a while. How England was *so cold, like winter, heh, Fadzai?* Even though it was 25C and everyone was in T-shirts and shorts. And why doesn't anyone in this place smile, as though all Zimbabweans went around with a huge grin on their faces?

She saw them before Sam did, but she didn't wave until he did. She gave them the customary greetings, curtseying before her in-laws with something like surrender and offering to carry Fadzai's bag. It was light. She wondered where she'd put the bag of mealie-meal and bottle of Mazoe orange she usually brought over in her hand luggage. Probably in her suitcase, she thought, spitefully. They never brought many clothes, expecting to be kitted out while they were here. She supposed that the near-empty holdall was for the ice-cream cartons. She wished briefly that she had at least three in the bin for Fadzai to find later that evening.

She thought Leonard and Fadzai were rather silent on the way home. They answered all Sam's questions but volunteered nothing themselves. They looked older, too, but more than

78

that: harassed, tired. The trip, she thought. At least it may keep them quiet. But the quietness persisted. They didn't seem to want to go anywhere. She left them at home more than once while she went shopping and, when they did come with her, they followed her around like faithful dogs, occasionally turning something over in their hands and then replacing it on the shelves. No mention of cost, no gasps of awe. Something was wrong.

'So many different types of bread!' Mary heard herself exclaiming at one point during a shopping trip, but Leonard just nodded and said, 'Yes, lots.'

When they went out for dinner, neither Leonard nor Fadzai seemed to want anything to eat. They went to bed early, they didn't talk to the neighbours or want anyone to come round.

'How's that huge estate of yours you call a garden?' she heard Mike Robson ask Leonard once over the wall.

'Oh, fine, fine,' Leonard answered dejectedly and didn't pursue the subject.

The night before they were due to return, Mary was back late from shopping. She'd been buying them small gifts to take back with them. The hallway was dark and she flicked on the light switch with a strange sense of trepidation. She couldn't hear anything: no voices, no television, no radio. Only the distant sounds from the street. She would have called 'Hello', but something stopped her and she carefully turned the handle of the lounge door, which was never usually closed. Inside it was dark except for the yellow glow of a small lamp on a side table. Leonard was standing facing the wall, his shirt pulled halfway up his back, while Sam examined him. Fadzai hovered anxiously near. Mary felt that familiar twinge of exclusion that she often felt when she saw all three of them together, and yet this time there was something different too. Something else. She closed the door.

Sam was already asleep when she got into bed later that night. She tried reading for a bit and then gave up; she couldn't concentrate.

'Sam,' she leant over him and nudged him gently. 'Sam.'

He grunted, but didn't open his eyes.

'Sam, is there something wrong? Your parents, I mean.'

He opened his eyes and turned over to face her. He took a deep breath as though he were about to reveal something, but merely said: 'There's no problem, Mary, none whatsoever. They're getting older, you know, we must remember that. They get tired.' He squeezed her hand, turned onto his back, and closed his eyes again.

'But what about the permits, the visas... you know, them coming to live here.'

He sighed, but kept his eyes closed. 'They're happy, Mary. In their own way, back in Zim, they're happy.'

But Mary wasn't happy. The next morning, she sat her in-laws down in the living room and addressed them directly.

'What's wrong?' she asked. 'Have we done something? Sam and I?'

'Nothing's wrong,' said Leonard, playing with the tassel on the crocheted armrest of the chair, a present Fadzai had brought over the last time and something Mary detested but had got out for their visit.

'There is something...'

'Nothing.'

They sat in silence for a long time before Mary finally said:

'Do you know Sam has applied for you to move here? To the UK?'

She waited for their reaction.

Nothing.

She became more insistent. 'We can find you somewhere to live.'

Nothing.

'I mean, you can live with us initially. The spare room...'

Leonard turned and looked at Fadzai who sat turning her hands in her lap.

'Very kind,' she said, 'very kind.'

Mary waited. She expected arms around her neck, tears of joy and relief, beers cracked open, the neighbours invited round, Leonard's voice booming across London.

'No, thank you.' The voice was almost a whisper. She leaned forward. Leonard spoke slowly: 'It's been turned down. We found out before we left.'

'Before you came... when? Sam? He didn't say.'

There was silence.

'We'll reapply,' she hazarded. 'There are ways...'

'No, thank you.' Fadzai's voice was quiet but determined. 'We really must be getting back.' Then momentarily her voice wavered. 'Zimbabwe – it's our home. No need to worry. We've got a big garden.'

'I'd like to go up to Whiteladies Road if you don't mind. I'd like to see it again.'

Martin tapped his boiled egg softly with a teaspoon exactly three times and then took a knife and sliced the top off. He dipped his spoon into the warm yellow crater and took a mouthful. He seemed to hold it in his mouth for a couple of seconds before swallowing it as though savouring an expensive wine. Then he took a pinch of salt from the small container on the table and sprinkled it over the egg. The taste being more to his liking, he pulled himself straighter and closer to the table in anticipation of a satisfying breakfast.

Madeline took a bite of her apple and watched her brother eat with interest. He was clearly a man of habit, but one whose routine had been set and monitored by a devoted wife for many years and, now that he was alone, he struggled to fulfil its requirements himself.

He had watched the egg boil as an anxious parent might sit at the bedside of a sick child waiting for a fever to break. He scooped it out of the water with such a sudden clumsy movement that it wobbled precariously and broke as he dropped it in the egg cup.

Now, as she watched him, she thought how like a little boy he looked, happy that he had made something by himself, but uncertain, too, and anxious for approval.

He looked up, a piece of toast in one hand. There was a spot of yolk in the corner of his mouth.

'Aren't you hungry?' He motioned to the apple which she held between thumb and forefinger. She shook her head.

'I hardly ever eat first thing. Just thought I'd keep you company.'

'I couldn't survive on that,' he said with a shrug, picking up his teacup and taking a sip. His eyes caught hers momentarily over the rim. He looked away and replaced his cup on the saucer.

Ignoring his comment, she said, 'You'll find it changed since you were last there. Whiteladies, I mean.'

'Is it? Full of immigrants, I expect. Every Tom, Dick and Harry wants to get in now.'

'That's not what I meant,' she interrupted, her words hard and brusque. 'It's been upgraded quite a bit. *Gentrified*. Full of wine bars and bistros. Charge the earth for a glass of wine.'

He raised his eyebrows in agreement and popped the last piece of toast in his mouth. Then he dabbed the corner of his mouth with a napkin. Irritated with his mannerisms, she stood up, tossed the apple core on his saucer and watched how he pulled in one corner of his mouth in disgust. She always used a mug; she had to dig in the back of her cupboard for the teacup and saucer he had asked for.

'I'm going to brush my teeth,' she said. 'You don't mind clearing up, do you?'

'No, no, of course not. Just wait for my food to go down.'

With her hand on the door handle, she closed her eyes shut for a second, took a deeper breath than usual and went out into the hallway.

In the bathroom, Madeline squeezed a length of toothpaste onto her brush. After all these years, she could still hear the note of irritation in her father's voice. *Just a pea-sized amount, Madeline. There's no need to use all that. Look at the mess for God's sake! The mess.*

Madeline looked at herself in the mirror. At sixty-five, her auburn hair was grey at the roots and needed a good cut, but she never seemed to find the time to go to a hairdresser. In all likelihood she would get the hell in and do it herself one Saturday afternoon. It didn't matter if it weren't quite straight at the back: it was always tied into a bun. It was messy. It always had been messy, but she liked it. The bohemian look.

As a young woman in the '70s, she hadn't worn make up, citing beauty as one of the demands society placed on women. She sent letters of protest to the big cosmetics companies who tested their products on animals and had once spent a night outside Boots to remonstrate their use of lanolin in their hand creams.

Indeed, most of her life she had hailed the virtues of natural beauty, washing her face with nothing more complicated than a bar of soap. This is me, this is who I am, she would say. What you see is what you get. As she had got older and the clichés had failed to give sustenance to her battle cry, she had given in to wearing a light foundation to cover the broken red veins on her cheeks, a lick of mascara and a thin line of lipstick if she was going out. She applied this now, leaning closer to the mirror as she did so. She hesitated a moment before drawing back, noticing the puffiness round her grey-green eyes. Then she scooped her hair into a straggly bun, flicked the fringe out of her eyes and left the bathroom.

Her bedroom was a cacophony of colour: bright orange, red and yellow cushions with lots of tassels and beads were strewn across a large, untidy bed covered with a voluminous blue throw embroidered with flowers and elephants and inlaid with pieces of mirror. Various handbags and scarves hung from the end of the brass bedstead and an overflowing pine cupboard was pushed closed by a chair on which reposed a number of files and textbooks. Thrust right into the corner, so close to the bed that there was no room for a separate stool, was a small dressing table. It was covered in jewellery and little boxes and the ends of burnt incense sticks. In the middle of it all was a photograph of a cat in a silver frame. She chose a scarf, squirted a light floral perfume on her wrists and looked for her bag.

She could hear Martin in the bathroom and imagined him squeezing out the toothpaste to the exact requirements of their father. He would wet his comb and draw his hair back in the same way, leaving little ridges visible on the sides. Then he would splash on just a smidgeon of eau de cologne, wash his hands and dry them vigorously, one finger at a time, making sure he left the towel hanging exactly in the middle of the rail.

A memory rose up momentarily: the smell of her father in the morning when she entered the bathroom. An overbearing masculine scent that stopped her at the door. She remembered how she would hesitate as though an invisible something blocked her way and then, pressing herself against the door frame, she would skirt inside. As a teenager, she became defiant and smoked there every evening, sitting on the side of the bath, her back against the wall, the door shut and the window open. When she was twenty-five, her father died and she spent four hours cleaning the bathroom with bleach, scrubbing each nook and cranny with a fierce determination. His cologne she left in the medicine cabinet and it was only six years later, when her mother died, that she worked up the courage to throw the bottle away.

Perhaps because he was a man, Martin had not seemed to need to shake off his father in the way she had done. She didn't imagine he gave him much thought. For all her brother's brains and success in business, he was not the contemplative type. In fact, he was a stickler for tradition in the same way that she abhorred it. His daughters had done well at school and got first-class degrees. Teresa was now a lawyer in London and Samantha a lecturer in Business Administration at Rhodes University in South Africa. They were nice enough girls; she had met them a couple of times, but they didn't have much in common with her and contact had been sporadic.

And then Martin came to stay.

She remembered the day he had phoned. It was on one of the hottest days that summer. The air outside was positively shimmering in the heat but she was in the kitchen, wrestling with a roast, which she now regretted having started. Her temples and armpits were wet with sweat and she mopped her face with a tea towel before answering the phone.

'Hello?' she answered, slamming the tea towel on the back of a chair, aware of the barely masked irritation in her voice. She thought it would be good for putting off any cold callers. The last thing she needed at this precise moment was double-glazed windows.

There was a pause and a slight crackle. Her first instinct was to put the phone down, but then she hesitated. 'Hello?'

Suddenly his voice was loud and near. 'Madeline? Hello. It's Martin.'

After all these years. She had stood quite still as he had told her in his inimitably direct manner how his wife Bridgette had been diagnosed with Alzheimer's a year ago, how her condition had rapidly declined and was now such that she didn't recognise him or her daughters anymore.

'It's not good,' he said. 'We need to get her some help. There's nothing here.'

Here was Zimbabwe, a place he had moved to fifty years previously when it was still called Rhodesia, a rebel country dominated by a white minority government.

She could still remember him standing at the front door, a young man of twenty-one, an overnight bag in hand, tall and upright, his dark hair combed back leaving little ridges in its wake.

She remembered how he had ruffled her hair, how she had choked back the tears, how he had looked away and never looked back. Father had shaken his hand and clasped his shoulder in what was his attempt at an embrace and Mother had kissed his cheek and then, placing her hand there, had told him to be good and to write soonest. Then the taxi, into which Martin's trunk had already been loaded, beeped impatiently, and a minute later he was gone.

There had been letters at first and postcards. He had written dutifully every week, telling them of the rooms in which he lived, of his no-nonsense landlady who made him a full English breakfast every day, of his job as a trainee mining engineer. Father had found the placement for him through his acquaintances at the Club.

Then there was news of a girlfriend.

'Fool,' said Father, throwing the letter down on the breakfast table. Madeline picked it up and wiped egg yolk off the back page. 'He's young. He should play the field.'

'Sow his wild oats, you mean?'

'Exactly.'

'Like I'm allowed to do?'

'Madeline,' warned her mother primly from the end of the table. 'You know you mustn't speak to your father like that.'

'You're a girl!' exploded her father, banging his fist down on the table, making the cutlery jump in a spasm of metal on metal. 'It's different, for God's sake. I've told you. It's different!'

Madeline picked up a short denim jacket from the back of a chair, arranged the scarf around her neck and then fished her purse out of her handbag, checking to see how much cash she had. Satisfied, she slipped it back in.

'You ready?' she called.

'Just get my jacket,' he replied, walking down the stairs, holding onto the rail at the same time. He was still a good-looking man she thought. A little stooped now and not quite so agile, but he had looked after himself – or somebody else had at least – and had maintained his athletic build. Not like her, she thought ruefully, sucking in her stomach. She had, as her father had chosen to remark on his deathbed, taken after her mother's side of the family who had all run to fat before the age of twenty-five.

She shut the door behind them with a bang and dropped the key in her bag, zipped it up and started walking with a brisk vehemence. Martin had been folding down the collar of his jacket, which was a dark navy cotton of the ilk she associated with pompous Conservative types who owned yachts and read *The Telegraph*, and had to run to catch up with her.

'Whoa there. What's the rush?'

'There should be a bus at the end of the next road in about three minutes.'

'And if we miss it?'

'There's another one three minutes later.'

'Exactly.'

'I don't like waiting.'

'Beats having a heart attack getting there.'

She slowed down. 'Sorry.'

'It's fine. I've just forgotten how quickly people here walk.'

'Do we?'

'There's not enough time is there? Everyone's rushing God knows where.'

'I hadn't noticed. Anyway, people have things to do and no one to help. Jobs to go to.'

'You don't.'

The words stung. 'Not now. I did.'

He didn't answer and she interpreted his silence as a refutation of her words. It was true that she hadn't had a paying job for a long time, but it wasn't as if she had done nothing with her time. Undertaking a full-time degree as a mature student had been the most difficult thing she had done in her life. She had enjoyed it: it was fascinating, exhilarating, but hard. She had struggled to keep up with the younger students, often taking more time than was generally allowed to complete assignments and she had opted to re-sit two examinations for which she had received low grades. A year after finishing her degree, she signed up for a part-time Master's, but had yet to finish all the modules. In between she had done two creative writing courses and an online counselling course. Now she considered changing her Master's from social work to history of art.

'Did Bridgette ever work?'

There was a dig in her words and she couldn't help feel a pang of guilt for picking on Bridgette, a woman who sat in a nursing home, not knowing what time of day it was or who her children were or why this man who called himself her husband appeared once a week with flowers and a slab of Cadbury's dairy milk chocolate.

At the same time, Madeline knew Martin wouldn't feel the dig. That his wife hadn't ever worked was not a criticism in his eyes.

'No, she didn't. She had the girls, of course. Kept her out of mischief.'

Madeline felt another shiver of irritation. The patronising inferences of such comments riled her.

'Maybe,' she ventured, aware of a gentle heat at the base of her neck, where she always felt her anger first, 'maybe she should have got up to mischief.'

He looked sideways at her. 'What do you mean?'

She shrugged, initially backing down from supporting her comment and then, with a slight spring forward so she was again a step ahead of him, she said: 'Well, it's only that we hear so much about keeping ourselves active. Especially the brain; it needs a challenge.'

'I see. Can you slow down? I'm sorry, but I really am struggling to keep up with you.'

'You drive everywhere over there, don't you? I remember you said once.'

'More than here, yes.'

'Everyone has a car?'

'Well, not everyone, no.'

'Just white people.'

'White people? No, of course not. Whatever gave you that idea?'

She shrugged again. It wasn't her territory. She saw the bus swing slowly onto the top of the road and sped up again.

'Come on. We don't want to miss this one.'

They reached the bus stop in time and she stuck her arm out into the road as it approached. She unzipped her bag and took her bus pass out, flashing it to the bus driver as she clambered on. Martin brought a handful of coins out of his pocket and counted them out. The bus lurched forward and he stumbled sideways, dropping a couple of the coins as he did so. The ticket machine buzzed, he tore off the strip of paper and followed her to an empty seat.

'Worth getting one of these,' she said, waving her pass at him, before putting it back in her bag.

'Yes,' he sniffed, shifting sideways so that he could slip the remaining coins back in his pocket. 'I suppose I should milk the system as much as I can now I'm here.'

'Milk the system? It's a bus pass. You're entitled to one when you're over sixty.'

'Entitled. That's the key word. Everyone's entitled – because of their age or their sex or their disability – or inability – or their race or their colour.'

She fought back an overwhelming desire to take him to task.

'I take it you don't have them in Rhodesia. Bus passes.'

'Zimbabwe, please. No, we don't. And it's not because we all have cars either. It's not a welfare state; there's no cosseting. No one to look after you.'

'You sound proud.'

'Not at all. There's nothing more frightening than a life without a safety net to catch you when you fall. I've seen too many people dive off the high wire. No pension, no savings, no income. It's a long way down.'

She didn't answer him. He had told her all of this on a couple of occasions. The farm invasions, the hyper-inflation, the shortage of goods. He said life had been hard; they had lost their savings and the stress, he believed, was partly to blame for Bridgette's condition. Yet Madeline found it difficult to imagine. She'd always thought he had done quite well. Surely he would have investments set aside and various nest eggs to provide an income in his retirement? It just didn't make sense for him to have nothing.

She turned to the window and watched the streets pass by. It was an overcast late September day; not cold yet – perfect for a walk up Whiteladies Road, even though its wine bars and estate agents and overpriced speciality shops didn't interest her. She wondered if he would mind her taking a diversion into Cotham. It was the part of Bristol she liked most, probably because it hadn't changed very much. She loved the rows of hippy shops and vegetarian cafes: unusual little places tucked away from the sprawling commercialism of the giant supermarket chains and high street shops.

'I'll show you a shortcut home on the way back. In case you come this way by yourself.' There was a note of generosity in her voice as though she were letting him in on a local secret. Inwardly, she felt a flutter of panic; would he think she was suggesting he could stay on with her?

'The nursing home is this way, isn't it?'

'Yes. It's not far from Whiteladies.'

'Good. I'm getting my bearings.' He smiled and she looked away again, embarrassed but not knowing why.

A few minutes later, turning from the window, she said to her brother: 'We'll get off at the next stop.'

They walked along without speaking. As the houses gave way to shops and offices, Martin became absorbed with looking through windows and staring up at the architecture of various buildings that caught his fancy, unaware of people and pushchairs and cyclists who streamed around him in a constant flow. His was the oblivion of the tourist who sees only himself, the pivotal figure around which everything else revolves and to whom everything demurs. She kept quiet, allowing him to explore on his own, refraining from providing a running commentary on everything she knew.

Outside an estate agent, he stopped and read through every property advertised whilst she walked a little way ahead and spent a disproportionate amount of time reading newspaper hoardings outside a newsagent's. He rejoined her, shaking his head and commenting on the high price of property.

'You looking to buy?'

'Absolutely not. I'd never afford it.'

'Oh.' She was surprised but didn't pry any further. They hadn't discussed much about his future.

Outside a pâtisserie, he stopped, his eyes taking in the rows of cakes, tarts, chocolate eclairs, croissants and other delicacies arranged in the window.

'Pâtisserie!' he scoffed. 'Why don't they just call it a bakery?'

'Because it's not?'

'Yes, it is.'

'Let me assure you that we wouldn't have had anything like that when we were growing up. Apple pie was just about as exotic as it got.'

'Nothing wrong with apple pie,' he said, walking on and then stopping almost immediately. His face had assumed the look of a detective on the brink of solving a mystery. He glanced up and down the street, gently nodding his head in confirmation of whatever he was thinking.

'This was a greasy spoon.' He motioned to the Italian restaurant next to the pâtisserie. 'I'm ninety-nine point nine per cent sure. Do you remember coming here with Dad and Uncle Bill on a Saturday morning?'

She shook her head. 'I was probably helping Mum with the hoovering.'

Her remark went by unnoticed, so completely was he absorbed in the comparison of past and present.

'There were two ladies, sisters, who ran it for many years. One was very large,' – he demonstrated her width with his hands – 'and the other very, very thin.'

'I remember them. We used to call them the Spratts.'

'Did we?'

'They weren't sisters. They were a lesbian couple.'

'Really? Were they?'

'They were. I only found out years later. They called

themselves sisters so they could get away with living together.'

'I must say it does surprise me.'

'Why? Did you expect them to look a certain way?'

'No, no. Of course not. Anyway, just about every second person seems to be gay these days. They seem perfectly okay, live a respectable life and then one finds out they're as queer as a nine-bob note.'

'I can see why you feel so let down. All that respectability must be quite misleading.'

His attention was already drawn to the next building and she could sense his dismissal of the subject. She felt another twinge of guilt for she knew her main reason for mentioning it was to aggravate him.

What was he looking for, she wondered? A trip down memory lane with everything exactly how it was fifty years ago? He would be disappointed, she knew, as he had been disappointed with everything else since arriving: hair styles and manners, traffic, the news, pedestrians, the fashion of the young, prices that were too high in some cases (train tickets) and too low in others (frozen meals, which he deemed indicative of the withering of family values).

It wasn't as though he hadn't seen the changes over the years. He had been back at least four times since he left, although once was just at a restaurant at Heathrow where he had been in transit to Turkey on business.

She had taken along her boyfriend at the time, Clive. They were both thirty but looked seventeen with their long hair, leather jackets and thigh-length boots. Clive kept a small tin of tobacco in his pocket and smoked roll-ups, which she could see Martin disapproved of. He ordered a pint of Snakebite and made some terrible joke about it being an apt choice when meeting someone from Africa. Martin had smiled weakly and ordered a half bottle of Beaujolais to go with his smoked salmon and rocket salad.

When the waiter returned and said that they didn't serve Snakebite, Martin simply said, 'Oh dear. Is there anything else you would like?' and she had resented the patronising tone in his voice. What was worse was that he wasn't aware of it.

'Do you want a drink?' he asked when they were about halfway up the hill.

'It's a bit early, isn't it?'

'Coffee. There must be somewhere to have a nice cup of coffee.'

'Costa? It's not far.'

'Is it a chain? I don't want a chain.'

They found a small place a few doors up. A bit pricey, she thought as her eyes scanned the menu, but she assumed he was paying. Whatever his faults, he was generous and it was doubtful he would have abided a woman paying the bill, even if that woman was his sister.

She ordered a Tanzanian, he a Costa Rican.

'Had enough of Africa,' he said, pushing out his bottom lip.

'Not going back?'

He shook his head. 'Doubt it. Nothing to go back to now.'

'Is it all sold?'

'Lock, stock and barrel.'

She remembered the photos of the large house with a swimming pool and tennis court.

'They're making huge advances into Alzheimer's treatment,' she began, although she wasn't sure why she said it. Perhaps to make him feel better. 'It's amazing what can be done.'

He shrugged. 'Too late, unfortunately.' He looked away, pulling his lips together. He began to hum.

The coffee arrived. He smiled his appraisal at the waitress who placed two cafetières and two over-sized cups on the table. She stood back with the air of one who has just completed a magic trick and then headed off in the direction of new customers.

'Don't you think,' Madeline started on a different tack. 'Don't you think it was odd that Father frequented a greasy spoon?'

'Why?'

'Well, because of what he was like. Uncle Bill, I can understand, but Father just wasn't the type.'

'What's the type?'

'Well… you know.'

'Working class?'

'Yeah, well, I don't like to think in terms of class. It's old-fashioned… limiting.'

'What would you call it then?'

She clenched her fists in frustration, bringing one down rather heavily on the table. It was the first time that day that he seemed to notice something she had said or done.

'I don't know. I don't know. He just wasn't the type, that's all. Nothing to do with his *class*. More the way he thought about himself. He worked in an office, had a mortgage and belonged to a *club*.'

'It wasn't a club in the way you're thinking of. It was just an ex-servicemen's club. Nothing fancy.'

The coffee was hot and burnt her throat. She replaced the cup on the saucer.

'He dressed up to go to it and it was a men's only affair. Mother never went, except for the Christmas dinner.'

'That doesn't mean anything. It really wasn't that special. Everyone dressed up back then.'

She watched him take a sip of his coffee, draw his lips back, swallow and then take another sip.

'Hot,' he said, putting it down. 'Tasty though.'

Mildly annoyed, she shook a sachet of sugar vigorously, tore the end off and tipped the contents of the packet into her coffee.

'Where do you want to go next?'

'You have a lot of sugar,' he noted, ignoring her question. 'Do you know sugar has been linked to Alzheimer's?'

She blew noisily out of her mouth and he looked at her in surprise. A long strand of hair fell in front of her eyes and she looped it back over her ear.

'I thought we'd go to Cotham. It's not far from here. I love it. It's my favourite part of town.'

'Cotham? Don't remember it.'

'We cycled there once, don't you remember? You bought a Cliff Richard LP and I got a Harry Belafonte single.'

He rolled his head backwards slightly and thought a moment. 'Yes, I remember now. Young Ones. You got into trouble for not asking if you could go.'

'I always got into trouble.'

He laughed and stirred his coffee again. '*And young ones*

shouldn't be afraid,' he sang softly. 'Didn't you go into your bedroom and refuse to come out?'

'For two days.'

'To live, love, while the flame is strong. For two days. A self-defeating protest.'

'I didn't mind.'

'For we may not be the young ones very long. We played it on our fortieth wedding anniversary.' His eyes dropped to his cup and he sat back with a big sigh. 'Teresa just put it on my iPod for me.' He shook his head. 'I don't listen to it much.'

She had been twisting the empty sugar sachet round her finger. Now she tossed it into the saucer and unzipped her bag. 'Shall we get the bill?'

'Yes, sure.' He waved to a waitress. 'I'll get it. Don't worry.'

'Thank you.' She zipped her bag again. 'I'll just pop to the ladies.'

When she came back, Martin was chatting amicably to the waitress. He was still a charming man and had a way of handing out compliments that was neither corny nor creepy.

'She's from Poland,' he said as they stood on the step of the coffee shop.

'Is she?' She pulled on her jacket, re-arranging her scarf and slinging her handbag strap over her shoulder.

'Working to send herself to university.'

'All going to come to an end soon, isn't it? With this Brexit crap.' She undid her bun, scraped her hair back and tied it up again.

'Mind you,' he said, walking up the road with a renewed jauntiness in his step, 'there are too many of them here. It has got a little crazy.'

'Too many of whom exactly?'

'Immigrants. It's unsustainable.'

'And you don't see yourself as an immigrant?'

'Absolutely not I was born here. I'm British.'

'Some would argue with you over that. You've lived away for most of your life. Why should you now come and claim benefits?'

He stopped in surprise and looked sharply at her. 'Is that what you think? You think I'm here to bum off the state like any other refugee from God knows where.'

'Where?'

'Africa, Asia.'

'And the Poles.'

'What?'

'You didn't mention the Poles.'

'So? They're not refugees.'

'Because they're white?'

He shook his head as though she had completely lost the plot.

'Let's just leave it.'

'No, no. Come on. Let's have it out.'

He started walking ahead of her. 'For goodness sake, Madeline. You're accusing me of being a racist. Bridgette's carer is a Nigerian. She's attentive, she's clean, she's chirpy – which is more than I can say for some of the English staff.'

They walked along in silence, she lagging behind. At the junction with Aberdeen Road, she stopped. 'I'd like to go to Cotham. Are you coming?'

He didn't answer. He was turned away from her, standing with his hands in his pockets and leaning back on his heels.

'We could have lunch.'

'No,' he said, turning towards her and rubbing his forehead with one hand. 'I'm going to pop in on Bridgette. I... would you like to come?'

She hesitated.

'Not this time if you don't mind.' And then as an afterthought, 'I'm looking for some essential oils. Lavender and ylang ylang. Can't get them anywhere else.'

Her words lay like a heavy dark blanket between them. He nodded.

'You've got a key, haven't you?'

He nodded again.

'And you know the bus, don't you? Number three all the way or get a ten and then cross the road and get a twenty-seven.'

'Right.'

'Right,' she hesitated. 'See you then.'

He nodded and turned, carrying on up the hill, but he had only gone a little way before he was back.

'You never came.'

'What?'

'To visit. You never came.'

'I...'

'All those years we never saw each other.'

'I didn't have the money.'

'Please don't.' He stopped her with his hand.

She shifted uneasily. 'I just didn't agree with it all.'

'Didn't *agree*? With what?'

'You being there. In Africa. As a white man.'

'Oh, for crying out loud...'

'It was wrong going out there. Changing someone else's culture.'

'Madeline, Zimbabwe has been independent for thirty-seven years. It has a black president – or haven't you heard?'

She shrugged, feeling out of depth. 'Still.'

'You haven't a clue, have you?'

He turned again to go. It was her turn to call him back.

'You never came for their funerals. Dad's or Mum's. You never came.'

He stopped. 'I'm sorry,' he said at last.

'Why couldn't you stand up to him?'

'Who?'

'Dad. Why is it you could never stand up to him?'

'What do you mean?'

'Going to the colonies. It was his idea. It was what one did – and you just went along with it.'

'Oh, for God's sake, Madeline.' His face was grey and drawn. 'It was you who could never get away. You baited him continuously, you egged him on. All you ever wanted was justification for your anger. I took my opportunity and I left.'

'And you didn't take me with you.' Her throat was tight with tears as she rubbed a hand up and down her shoulder.

'No, I didn't. I couldn't.' His voice dropped, became softer. 'I'm sorry.'

She nodded and turned and stumbled down the road in the direction of Cotham Hill. He didn't follow and she was glad. At the end of the road, she sat on a bus stop bench and searched for a tissue in her bag. Not finding one, she wiped the back of her hand across her cheeks and took a few deep breaths. She got her pass out and hailed the next bus, hoping it was going back towards Queens Road.

The bus moved in hard, jerking staccato as it fought its way through the traffic. She put out her hand to steady herself and fell forward instead. She had a strong, unnerving sensation that she was free-falling through a great cavern of rushing air, the bottom of which was years away. She was aware of her arms flailing stupidly and a strange yelp escaping from her throat. Then quite suddenly, she came to a halt, hitting her head on the seat in front. Tears of indignation welled in her eyes. A lady in the opposite seat leaned across and touched her hand.

'Are you all right?'

Madeline nodded and attempted a brief, lopsided smile. She felt suddenly old, suddenly useless, suddenly alone.

She let herself into the house, dropping her bag and key on the table in the hall. She took off her jacket and draped it across the newel post at the end of the staircase. Then she made her way slowly up to the bathroom and closed the door behind her. Thin, sad cobwebs of mascara hung about her eyes and the broken red lines on her cheeks rose up like tiny rivers of blood blooming on a pale, barren landscape.

From a washbag in a cupboard under the sink, she took a large pair of scissors. They were cold and their blades blunt, but she grabbed handfuls of hair and chopped her way through them. Chunks landed in the basin, on the floor; some got in her mouth and in her eyes. But she still went on cutting until all that was left stood in uneven clumps that she couldn't cut any shorter.

About seven, she heard Martin return. She heard him start up the first two stairs and then stop and go into the kitchen. She was lying on her bed, the cover pulled over her. She was tired, more than tired. Exhausted. She heard him switch on the radio and wondered what he was making for supper. Tomorrow. There would be tomorrow to explain, to talk. Perhaps to reconcile. But for now, she slept.

THE QUEUE

From her window, Mrs Atkinson looked out across the garden. The yellowing rag of a lawn stretched down to the washing line, and beyond that lay the vegetable garden. This itself was little more than a blur on her horizon, short-sighted as she was. It was hot. The air was dry with the fierce heat of summer. A film of sweat lay cool across her skin. She ran her tongue absently along her top lip, tasting the saltiness with exhaustion.

It was half past two on a Saturday afternoon, too hot still to go outside. A quietness had descended and stilled the house. Perhaps it was stupid to think it quieter than any other day? She lived alone – why should today be any different to any other day of the week? Yet there did seem to be a different feeling about Saturday afternoons; it was as though the whole world was quiet.

She turned the tap on and let the water run into a plastic bucket. It would be foolish to waste water at this time of year; the rainy season was never guaranteed. The water in the bucket could be used later. When the water ran colder, she filled a glass and raised it to her lips. Until then she hadn't realised how thirsty she was. She held the tap with one hand and continued to drink, all the time looking out of the window at the heat shimmering just above the lawn. She almost wanted to pour the water onto it and put out the white flames before they ate their way through more of the garden, their fingers drawing every drop of moisture from the earth.

There was a knock at the back door; it was Robinson, the gardener. He stood alongside his bicycle; it had once belonged to her son, Barry. Rose had given it to him the Christmas before last. He had been over the moon at the sight of it and had painted it shiny black and replaced the handlebars with those from a racing bike. He was smart in a light blue suit and white shirt. Rose felt hot just looking at him. His two-tone brogues were polished to a brilliant gleam and a ring on his right hand glinted brightly when it caught the sun. He had on a pair of sunglasses and a light blue hat that matched his suit. Robinson shifted the bike slightly and grinned apologetically at her. She knew what he wanted. It was the look he gave her when he wanted to borrow money.

'Yes, Robinson,' she said, waiting for the expected question, sipping the water patiently.

'Madam,' began Robinson, his grin expanding rapidly, 'please, I need to borrow some money for the weekend.'

Rose breathed deeply in and out. The silence of the afternoon seemed to breathe with her.

'What is it for this time?' she asked, although she didn't know why she bothered; she lent him the money no matter how strange or convoluted the reason was. Jack had criticised her for being too soft, but there was always a smile playing somewhere on his lips and sometimes he would ruffle her hair in a fatherly manner and kiss the top of her head. Jack. It all seemed such a long time ago.

'My brother has come from Kezi. He was promised a job down there' – here he pointed with his left hand towards the gate – 'in Riverside, but then the man said to him no job, so now he must go back to Kezi.'

Rose suddenly felt irritated. Was there a brother?

'You really must try and save your money,' she said crossly. 'I cannot afford to keep giving you loans all the time. I need money too.'

Robinson grinned, embarrassed yet certain he had won his way. Rose walked over to the kitchen table and took her purse from her bag, which was hanging over the back of a chair. She took out two hundred and fifty dollars and looked at it for a second. Putting the fifty back in her purse, she walked back to the door and handed him the two purply-blue notes. He had taken off his glasses and his eyes flickered over the money. He stood holding them, peeling one back as if to check there weren't more there. Immediately she knew it was not enough.

'Ah, madam,' he said with an apologetic laugh, 'it is now very expensive to go that side.'

Rose felt her body stiffen a little with irritation. How much more could it be? How much did she give him last Christmas to get home?

'How much is it now?' she asked. She could feel the heat from outside forcing its way in. She wanted him to go so that she could close the door and be alone in the relative coolness of the house.

'One thousand,' he said. Another laugh, another smile.

'One thousand!' she repeated, unbelievingly.

'Yes, it is one thousand now to go,' he replied.

Rose closed her eyes briefly, took a deep breath and went back to fetch her purse. She counted out a thousand dollars.

'That doesn't leave me a lot,' she said, 'so I must have this money back soon soon.'

'Yes, madam, I will bring it,' he said.

'Monday,' she said. 'I want it back Monday morning. First thing.'

'Yes, madam, I will bring it Monday,' he said.

He put the money she had just given him in the inside pocket of his jacket. Rose sighed and shook her head as she watched him cycle out of the gate. He started to whistle.

Rose wandered out into the garden. The earth was hard and dry. It had begun to crack in places, and looked as though it would fall apart if she walked on it and she would disappear into a great cavernous hole beneath. Even the rough, dry grass seemed to cling precariously to it; much of it was dead already. She could feel the heat on the back of her head and half turned to go in and fetch her hat when her eye caught sight of something strangely out of character with the rest of the garden.

Behind the washing line was the vegetable patch, but it had lain barren for months. Nothing seemed to grow and there wasn't enough water to keep anything alive. Next to the back fence, however, in a straight row, was a line of mealie plants. Rose stared at them in disbelief. Eight sturdy plants had pushed themselves triumphantly out of the earth and stood, as though ready for inspection, before her. The earth around them was dark and solid. It was not parched or cracked; it was warm, healthy earth that had been tilled and fed and looked after. A slight breeze jostled the mealies together, and their papery green arms lifted in a half wave. She could hardly see the white cobs, swaddled as they were in layers of thin green sheets. What looked like silvery flaxen hair tumbled down outside.

Rose looked at the scene in front of her in disbelief. So this was why he was always in the back garden when she called him. This was why the front garden looked unkempt and why weeds grew prolifically in the flowerbeds. She had noticed the deteriorating state of the garden but had thought it due to the late start to the rainy season and the poor soil in that area. She had meant to buy compost and fertiliser, but the actual act had constantly seemed to elude her. It was always on her shopping list, but somehow she always drove past the nursery and the garden centre without stopping. Something always made her drive on, and the items were added to the bottom of the next shopping list. If she was honest with herself, she would admit that she didn't see the point of caring any more what the garden looked like. How much longer would she be around? Isn't that what she thought every time she passed the nursery? Of course a good garden would add value to the house should Barry want to sell it, and he probably would. She doubted he would ever come back to Zimbabwe; there was no point, no future here for a young man and his family.

How different it was when she was his age! She remembered telling her mother they were going to Rhodesia. Jack had a job there, a good job, and the country was welcoming people. He told her of the lifestyle, the big houses and the gardens they had there, the servants, the weather. And now not one of those things would tempt Barry to come back. Her mother said she was a fool, and perhaps she was, but then she was young, and in love. Rose half smiled at the memory. Perhaps her mother had been right after all. You're wrong to marry an older man, she had said and shaken her head knowingly. You're making a big mistake. There's twenty years between you and him. What are you going to do when he is an old man and you still want to go places and do things? But we love each other, she had protested. Wasn't that the most important thing? Everything else should fall into place around that.

But perhaps her mother hadn't been thinking about whether they'd still be able to play tennis together in twenty years' time, or have the same friends and interests. Maybe she was talking about now, this time; retirement. Old age is so far away when you are young.

Rose suddenly felt an urge to rip out the mealies, cut them down with her bare hands and crush them into the earth. Her anger, however, was not directed at Robinson so much as the memory of her mother, sitting stiff-lipped through her wedding ceremony and resignedly kissing her afterwards; a dry, papery, unforgiving kiss. Resisting the urge to destroy Robinson's work, Rose turned abruptly and went into the garage. Here she searched through an array of gardening tools, many broken and rusty, for a small trowel and a rake. She would show him, she thought, she would show him who could and who could not grow flowers. Marching over to the flowerbeds in the front garden, she knelt down and furiously dug at the weeds. Over and over she tugged and pulled and lunged. A pile of weeds grew next to her, their long thin white roots exposed to the sky and the sun.

Although there wasn't a lot left in the beds after the weeds had been uprooted, Rose felt a deep sense of satisfaction. She turned on the tap and held the hose above the smattering of daisies and violets. There was even a rose bush she had never noticed, spindly and flowerless and dying. A rose by any other name would smell as sweet. Except you, Rose, my Rose, Jack always used to say. Oh Jack, where are you now?

That evening, Rose decided she would see to the front garden herself. Robinson could do all the watering and look after the back garden, which he would prefer anyway, and she would tend to the flowerbeds. She would go to the garden centre on Monday, buy a range of seedlings and perhaps a couple of potted plants – and what about a hanging basket, those were so beautiful – and she would spend the next couple of days digging and planting and watering.

She couldn't wait. The next day she prepared the beds. Not content with her work of the day before, she turned the soil over with the trowel and picked the dry leaves off what plants there were. Then she moved onto the next flowerbed and did the same. And the next. It was hard work. The sun was hot and she had to go back into the house for her large straw hat, but she could still feel the sun through her shirt, warm at first but growing more threatening and insistent. It didn't want her there; she was supposed to be hiding in the house like she always did, sad and alone, not out here actually enjoying herself. The sun resented her presence and despised her defiance; it would do anything to drive her away and so pressed itself harder against her, driving its spiteful fingers deeper.

Yet she did not give up. All day she worked until the beds were ready and the soil lay cool and dark and inviting and a pile of dead leaves and weeds had collected beside her. Then she went indoors and washed her hands. She stood at the kitchen sink and scrubbed her nails with a small brush. It was

111

then she thought *I need the money. I need the money I lent Robinson.* He wasn't back yet. She would wait until after she'd had something to eat for supper and then go and see if he was in. With an air of accomplishment, she started to prepare the meal. She took two eggs out of the fridge and set them down on the counter. Normally she would just boil them and have them with a slice of bread and butter and perhaps a piece of cheese. It was so expensive now that she only allowed herself a small slice, however hungry she was. But then she was never hungry, not these days. She had watched herself getting thinner and thinner over the past year. Her pension didn't go far these days. Don't worry, Jack had said, I've a great pension. We'll even be able to travel. Perhaps even go to Europe every couple of years. Europe! When had she last been there? Rose thought for a moment. She had gone to France as a child with her father. She remembered sitting with him in a café in Nice. It was a brief memory; she remembered him reading the paper and her looking out of the window at the people walking by. It was raining and they had eaten hard dry bread and drunk coffee while they waited for it to pass. Ever since then the smell of coffee made her think of rain.

They had never gone to Europe, she and Jack. They hadn't gone anywhere after he retired, except Nyanga once at the start of Jack's illness. After that he had rapidly gotten worse and then... well, what was the point of going on holiday on one's own? Her cousin Penelope did though. She sometimes got a postcard from her, normally from some Mediterranean country or other, and once one from Australia. She went on those Saga holidays, especially designed for people over fifty. Rose had laughed at first. Was fifty the cut-off point then? No mountain climbing or deep-sea diving! Penelope would never come and see her though, although she had promised to many times. She had once suggested that she and Rose meet in Cairo and tour the Middle East together. *You're already in Africa,* she had written, *it would save you flying all the way here if we could meet in Cairo. My neighbour, Sandra, went last year and she highly recommends the tour. It may sound expensive, but it does include all coach and air transfers and all the accommodation in Egypt and Israel.* Rose smiled ruefully at the memory of her cousin's letter. How could she tell her that Jack's pension barely paid the bills, never mind covering an eight-day tour of the Middle East. Penelope had always envied Rose for moving away, had always thought she and Jack lived some luxurious life in Africa. She thought Rose turning down the offer to join her in Cairo a sign of fear, the fear of being on one's own after years of being pampered and looked after by a generous and adoring, but much older, husband. *You HAVE to come here!* she had written from Australia, where she had managed to see Barry. They had written a joint postcard, Penelope's scrawl filling most of it and Barry adding a line of: *Hope to see you soon!* Although he knew jolly well she could never afford the trip.

Why doesn't he pay for you to go over? someone had once asked her. Oh, he's got his own life now, she had laughed in reply, I don't want to be a burden. Still, she had seen the accusing look in their eyes, the eyes of all the pensioners left behind. Children in England, in America and Australia. New Zealand, Canada, South Africa. Children brought up on sunshine and space and maids and a good education. Where were they now? They had thrown the country back in their parents' faces and run. I gave him the world, Rose once thought of Barry, and he had given it back in a smaller box, instead.

Rose made an omelette, a cheese omelette with a small side salad. She wished she had something to drink, a glass of wine perhaps, or a gin and tonic. Instead she poured herself a glass of water from a bottle in the fridge; she had long ago stopped buying fruit juices and, long before that, alcohol. But today was celebration enough. Her roughened hands could not have given her more joy to look at if they had held a glass of champagne, and the meal itself, the extra time she had spent making it, awakened in her a sense of life she hadn't felt for years.

That night she could hardly sleep. She woke twice, once just before dawn with a childlike feeling of excitement. Something was going to happen that day, something special. It was like Christmas, except that Christmas hadn't felt like this for a long time. Not since Barry had grown up, and really even before then when she had been a child. For the first time in a while, Rose deliberated over what to wear. Usually her wardrobe varied between two pairs of trousers and two blouses. Today, she pushed these well-worn garments along the rail and looked at what else she had. She looked right at the back of the cupboard where her evening dresses hung in plastic covers. She lifted one out and ran her hand along the fabric. Although it smelt a little stale, it was clean and soft and it hadn't faded at all. Rose smiled and pulled the dress a little closer to her. When had she last worn it? Years and years and years ago, yet when she held it she could remember all the feelings, as though it were just yesterday.

She used to have her wedding dress too, but had eventually given it away. She wondered if anyone still had it, or whether it had been thrown away or cut up and used for something else. She hadn't wanted to part with it, but what was the point really of keeping it? She had had no daughters, no one to give it to. When Barry got married to Anneline, she had thought briefly of giving the dress to her daughter-in-law, but had thought the style might be considered old-fashioned, and so had refrained from offering it, not wanting to embarrass the young girl who might have felt obliged to wear it.

She was a nice young girl, well, woman now, Anneline, thought Rose as she searched through her wardrobe for something suitable to wear. She had gone to stay with them in Cape Town about a year before they left for Australia. She hadn't known then of their plans and they didn't tell her. Rose stopped suddenly and looked up. What had they said? They had been talking in the kitchen in lowered voices and she had walked in. What had they been speaking about to make them start like that when they noticed her presence? Rose shook her head and carried on with her search. She eventually decided on navy blue skirt and a white blouse with a very thin navy line running through it. Jack loved her to wear navy; she hadn't wanted to wear it since his illness got so advanced he couldn't recognise her.

She sat at the dressing table and brushed her hair. Perhaps she should go for a cut, she thought. When had she last allowed herself that privilege? She looked at herself for a long time and then smiled. She was old, but she didn't look *too* bad. Thank god she had always worn a hat in the sun. Rummaging through a drawer, she found a pot of unused cream and some foundation. Anneline had given her the cream on her last visit. 'To cheer you up', she had said, but Rose hadn't used it. Slowly, she now rubbed it into her face and then smoothed a layer of foundation over it. She could still smell a faint perfume, even though it must have lain in the drawer for a good few years. How lovely it felt! How it awakened her and made her fingers tingle, like they had the day before when she had submerged them in earth and felt life, at first far away and then nearer, begin to beat again.

She was ready at last. She took another look at herself in the mirror and smiled. She straightened her posture and turned to look at herself from the side. Suddenly, she felt nervous. She hadn't dressed this way for ages. What if she bumped into someone she knew in town, something she invariably did? What would they think? That she had met someone new? That she had come into money? She sat on the edge of the bed and looked at her hands; she was sweating. For a moment her newfound confidence left her and she felt it was all a mistake. She would take these silly clothes off and change into her usual trousers and blouse, and she would take this silly make up off too.

It was the sudden vision of her old self, the downtrodden old woman, living out her last days in some sort of social and economic straitjacket, that made Rose change her mind yet again, and actually defy herself. She picked up her handbag and her car keys and, with a certain spring in her step, made her way to the kitchen. She opened the back door and called for Robinson. There was no reply. She called again, and still there was no reply. He hadn't come home the night before and he probably wasn't going to be at work that day. Rose's heart sank. Suddenly more than ever, she wanted to go into town. She looked in her bag. She had enough money to get some basic groceries and post a letter to Australia. She could always draw some money from the POSB while she was at the post office. She didn't do it often and, anyway, this was some sort of occasion. A memory of Christmas as a child briefly washed over Rose again. It was a feeling she wanted to hold on to and take with her, but it was gone. There was no reason why she should be so happy, except that she was alive and she had been dead for so long.

She started her car; it was nearly on empty. She would have to join a petrol queue on the way home. Normally she would have sighed and inwardly lamented the fact, feeling the realisation fall like a large stone into the well of sadness inside her. Today the fact that she had little petrol was a challenge: how far could she go? Rose giggled; this was called living on the edge in Zimbabwe. She reversed the Morris out of the gate rather more quickly than she was used to and felt her heart flutter in excitement.

All the way to town, she saw lines and lines of cars parked alongside the road. Many were left empty while their owners went to work. Some were parked at crooked angles, having obviously pushed their way into the queues. In places there were two or three lines of cars and, at one garage, a queue formed from both ends of the forecourt, causing chaos. A minibus full of commuters suddenly pulled out from the side of the road; it hadn't been in the queue but picking people up from a bus stop. Rose swerved into the next lane and a silver Land Cruiser shot by, its hooter screaming loudly at her. Rose clutched her chest and slammed on the brakes. The car behind her hooted as well and overtook, the driver leaning over and shouting at her. Fumbling at the gear stick, Rose slowly drove forward. Her heart was pounding and her palms were sweating.

She caught a glance at herself in the rear view mirror and was surprised at what she saw. Although she felt pale and frightened, her cheeks were still pink with rouge and her mouth red with lipstick. It made her feel better and she took a few deep breaths. She promised herself a cup of tea when she got to town.

She parked her car in the shade and decided she would try and walk as much as possible to conserve fuel. Perhaps she wouldn't bother getting any that day. There didn't look as though there was a lot about and she didn't want to wait in the sun for petrol that might not come.

Feeling rather important, she walked into the little café near the supermarket. She would have something to drink first and then go and do her grocery shopping. The café had changed hands many times since she had known it. For a long time it had been called Gregory's, after Tom Gregory, an Italian who had changed his name during the war in an effort to appear more 'English'. It was called Gregory's long after the old man had died in the late seventies, but it lost its feel, its certain something that made it special. Gradually it declined and became more of a takeaway than anything else and the name changed to Mr Tasty's, or was it Mr Yummy's, Rose couldn't remember. She hadn't gone there anyway. Then about five years ago, a young couple took it over and reopened it as a coffee shop once again. It was called Roseanne's, and had pretty floral tablecloths and chair backs, and the menus were printed nicely and there was a cappuccino machine and air conditioning in the hot summer months.

Rose hadn't been there for a long time, two or three years, and she noticed that there was now a carpet and they had repainted the walls; this time a light green. The waiter approached her with a menu but she shook her head and smiled.

'Don't worry, I know what I'm having. A cup of tea, please.'

The waiter laughed good-naturedly. 'Anything else?' His pen was poised above his notebook as he spoke.

'Nothing else,' said Rose, firmly. 'Just a nice big cup of tea.'

'OK,' said the waiter, putting his notebook away and removing some cutlery from the table. He polished a side plate with his cloth, looked up as two more customers walked in and went to show them to a table.

While Rose waited for the waiter to return, she got out her notebook and made a list of things she would need to buy in the supermarket. She didn't usually do this. If she forgot something, she forgot it and could do without it until the next week. But, today, she wanted to be organised; she wanted everything to go well. She wrote: eggs, milk, vegetables. Then she stopped, thought for a few seconds and added: yoghurt. She needed a treat. She also wrote sausages and instant pudding. She would spoil herself today.

The waiter returned a few minutes later with a teacup and saucer and a jug of milk. The cup was filled with hot water and a tea bag floated inside. Rose looked disapprovingly at it.

'Don't you give teapots these days?'

'You said you wanted a cup,' replied the waiter.

'Yes, I want a cup of tea, but usually you give a pot, not a cup.'

The waiter opened the menu and pointed to the section under 'Beverages'.

'You see, it says one cup here and one pot here.'

Rose looked. 'Is that the price?' she gasped. 'For one cup of tea?'

'Yes, madam, for one cup of tea, that is the price.'

Rose looked away. Her eyes were brimming with tears. How could she pay for the groceries now? Again, she tried to calm herself. She could always go to the POSB if she needed more money. She had decided on that before she left the house. Robinson still owed her money and she wouldn't have to come in again until next week. She tried to enjoy the tea and sipped it slowly, but really she just wanted to get out of the café and away from everyone.

She looked over at the table next to her. A young family was ordering coffee and cakes from the waiter. At another table, a man was eating breakfast. How much did all this cost? Where did they get the money?

Just as she was paying for her tea at the till, Rose felt a hand on her arm and a voice said: 'Rose! It is you! I was just walking past and I thought to myself, I'm sure that's Rose Atkinson, and it is! How wonderful to see you! How are you?'

It was Mabel Baker. Mabel and she had played tennis for years together. Mabel still looked as though she played.

'Mabel,' said Rose. 'How are you? Keeping well? That's good.'

'How are you?' asked Mabel again.

Rose nodded her head in response. 'Oh fine, fine, you know.'

There was a pause and then, 'You look really good, Rose. I'm so glad.'

Rose managed a half smile, but, she was thinking, she's surprised, surprised I look well, I expect she thought I was dead a long time ago.

Mabel squeezed her arm. 'It's a pity you're on your way out. We could have caught up over a cup of tea. And they do the most wonderful scones here.' She nodded over at the cashier who smiled. Rose could tell she was a regular. The invitation still hung on the air as Rose shook her head and said she must be getting on, she had so much to do. Mabel nodded her head and gave her an odd smile, as though she knew Rose didn't want to talk.

In an effort to appear as composed and as focused as possible, Rose went straight into the supermarket and picked up a basket. She forgot to go to the post office first. She had promised herself a leisurely wander of the shelves, something she used to enjoy doing, but now she put what she wanted into her basket and made her way to the till. The man in front of her was paying by cheque and she had to wait while the supervisor was called to approve it. Waves of heat swept over Rose and she shifted the basket from one hand to the other. She decided to take the things out and put them on the counter while she waited. It was only then that she remembered she hadn't gone to the post office. She tried to put the things back in the basket but the cashier had just started ringing her goods up on the till.

'Wait. Please,' said Rose. The man stopped.

'I haven't got enough money.'

The man stared.

'I forgot… I was supposed to go to the post office… Oh dear, I am sorry.'

The supervisor was called again. The story was explained. Rose apologised once more. Something was punched into the till and there was a whirring and a clicking and the receipt was torn off and signed and counter-signed. Her goods were placed to one side and Rose promised to be back in five minutes.

She hurriedly left the store and made a beeline for the post office. There was a queue. A notice written on what looked like the back of an advertisement for first day covers, and in writing that began in large capitals and ended in small, squashed letters, announced that one of the counters was closed. Rose waited. The heat washed over her again. This time the waves seemed larger, more threatening and insistent, determined to bring her down with them. The queue was moving slowly; people were withdrawing a lot of money and it wasn't even Christmas. Christmas. Did anyone still do that anymore? She remembered the card she had to send to Barry. Why did she keep it up, she suddenly thought? He never wrote, not even a card. Anneline always wrote it; she even signed it for him. Lots of love, Barry and Anneline. Anneline and Barry. What was it all about, anyway? All this loving, all this giving. Rose's head was spinning. She was hot, she was tired, she was flustered. All she wanted to do was sleep. She tried to calm herself. She was only two places from the counter. It wouldn't take long.

A man entered the post office. He was wearing torn blue overalls and broken shoes, and in his hand he carried his post office book. He walked up to the lady in front of her and said something to her. The woman stood back and let him go in front of her. Rose felt anger boiling up inside of her. She took two steps forward and pulled the man's arm roughly.

'What are you doing?'

He looked at her.

'I said, what are you doing?'

People were beginning to stare. The man turned back and faced the front. Rose pulled his arm again.

'Get to the back of the queue!'

He didn't move.

'I said, get to the back of the queue!' Her voice was strained to a high pitch.

'Get back! Get back!' she screeched. Everyone was looking. 'This is a queue, get back!'

The man didn't move so Rose turned on the man at the counter.

'Tell him to get in the queue!'

The man started to say something, but Rose could see he wasn't taking her side.

'The queue! The queue! Get to the back of the queue!'

Her heart was beating fast now and her palms were wet with sweat, but at the same time she was experiencing a feeling of letting go, of not caring. It was as if it were her privilege to scream and shout, as though she had been waiting for this moment all her life. The world started to spin and she felt slightly sick. It spun faster and faster and all she could hear was her voice on and on and on: 'The queue, go to the back of the queue!' She felt a pain somewhere, far away. Barry, she thought, and then, Jack. Darling Jack, where are you? She tried to steady herself and put out her hand. It was Anneline.

What was she doing here? Rose, she was saying, you mustn't creep up on us like that. You gave us such a fright. And there was Barry. He was smiling, but he looked worried, harassed. What had they been saying, just as she walked in? Something about Australia. Don't tell Mom, he said, it'll break her heart. What will, Barry, what will break my heart? But they had gone and there was only blue and then black and then nothing.

'Rose! Are you coming?' Jack's voice called up the stairs. 'We're going to be late!'

'Coming!' Rose called as she appeared at the top of the stairs, valise in one hand and hat and scarf in the other. She smiled excitedly when she saw Jack and then looked around for one last time, took a big deep breath and rushed down the stairs.

The car was waiting in the drive, the soft top rolled back for it was a beautiful summer day, the kind of day that shivers with excitement and anticipation. Jack took her valise and placed it in the boot. She squashed her hat on her head and turned to Jack with a grin.

He kissed her and started the engine. 'Ready?' he said.

'Ready.'

'Let's go!'

Her scarf streamed out behind her as the car shot off down the road.

In the darkened hospital room, Rose lay motionless except for an occasional jerk of her hand.

'I'm ready, Jack,' she whispered. 'I'm ready.'

LAST DRINK AT THE BAR

William Lloyd sat in the airport bar, watching the bubbles rise to the frothy top of his beer, lost in deep thought. He had lived in Cardiff for five years now and every year he looked forward to a brief return to his homeland, Zimbabwe, and catching up with all the guys there. He always went in August; it was his favourite time of the year: the time of year, in fact, when his dear old mum, now departed, had always sighed dreamily of spring and said, 'Wouldn't it be nice to go to the sea?' She never did, of course, but did it matter? When she died seven years ago in Edith Duly Nursing Home's frail care unit, she drooled consistently, ate jelly with a knife and fork and didn't even know what her own name was, never mind whether she had gone to the sea or not.

It mattered to William though. Never married, never had children. Alone. Lloyd saw his destiny stretched before him in one awful sweep: old age, senility, death. And not a soul to visit. Who would pay? The nursing home, the hospital, the funeral parlour? He had decided to do something about it. As much as he loved Bullies, as much as he was a Zimbo through and through, and as much as he would miss the sunshine and glorious blue skies of his home country, he feared, more than anything, an end at Edith Duly Nursing Home.

And so life found him tracing his roots. His mother was a Zimbabwean, well a Rhodesian really, but she didn't like to tell too many people: things can be so misconstrued, can't they? But her mother had been a Scot. William had a picture somewhere of a rather stern looking woman in a high collar and two long even more stern looking sweeps of hair piled up on her head. But this was far too tenuous a link for the British High Commission to grant him what he wanted. Luckily, his father had been born in Wales, leaving at the age of three for a sun-filled life in the colonies. It was through him that William was able to secure an ancestry visa. In another four years, he could apply for a British passport. Suddenly, the world was full of possibility and death did not hang too near. He had decided, too, to settle in his father's homeland, Wales. He could never quite get that picture of his great-grandmother out of his mind, imagining a Scotland populated with millions of her type. Wales was the place for him.

After all, there was Cardiff Arms Park, a name he much preferred to The Millennium Stadium, and where there was rugby, there was beer. And where there was beer, there were mates. Or at least so he thought. And there was the sea. Both were a disappointment. He tried pub after pub after pub after pub, but never did he find anywhere quite like The Bar in Bullies. The guys just weren't the same. He missed Boetie and Frickie and Leonard and Rookie. He even missed the barman, Nyoni, smartly presented every evening in his white shirt and black bow tie. He missed the jokes, the laughter, the philosophical discussions about the workings of a woman's mind. *Jusus!* He missed those guys.

And so every year, although he told himself he should spend his annual leave exploring his new country and maybe even take a drive up to Scotland, he found himself at Gatwick

Airport, eagerly awaiting his flight back home, having a few drinks and mentally having conversations with the guys about life in Mud Island.

The first time he went back was great. He didn't tell anyone; it was quite a surprise. 'Billy Boy!' they shouted as he walked into the bar. 'Howzit! Shit! You're looking white! Hey, Nyoni! You think we're white, look at this oan!' Hey, was it good to be back or what? He had stayed with Boetie and his wife and had a wonderful two weeks. Everyone was glad to see him, excited to hear all his news. What was life like in the UK? It must be so exciting. What had he done, where had he gone?

William had shaken his head wisely and told them.

'Aish, man, it's something else. You wouldn't believe it. *Variety!* Man, there's so much there.' He looked around at all the faces watching him. 'Beers? There are *hobos* of different types. Hobos. I don't think I've tried them all yet.'

'What else?' asked Frikie. 'I suppose you can buy anything you want?'

'*Anything*, my boet, *anything.*'

'So've you bought your own place, hey, I suppose?' asked Boetie, nodding his head as though it were a done fact.

'Ah, not quite, not quite. Still looking, you know.'

'What, you might want to move?'

'Well, just looking, that's all.'

'Maybe he's found himself a wife,' laughed Frikie, throwing his head back and drinking his third beer of the evening. Billy had been so kind as to buy the guys a few rounds. They all laughed, William not quite as hard as the others.

'Ach, no man,' he said, waving away the suggestion.

'What, no one for you there either, Billy?' Frikie continued. 'I thought you got lot of *variety*.'

Billy thought he could detect a slight sneer in Frikie's voice, but he ignored it.

'No, man, they're all into this woman's lib,' he answered, rolling his eyes as though that explained everything. The guys all nodded in sympathy.

'Yep,' said Boetie pulling his lips in and letting them go with a smack. 'That's what the modern world's coming to nowadays, isn't it?'

They all nodded in sad agreement.

'But, aish, you're so lucky things are cheap there,' said the quiet Leonard suddenly. Again they all nodded. 'You can buy a house and a car and washing machine and whatever, hey, and you've only been there a year!'

William started to say this wasn't actually true. In fact, he didn't own any of these things, but he stopped and kept quiet.

'*Ja*, man, what kind of car you got?' asked Rookie, looking expectantly at him.

William hesitated again before saying, 'Ford Sierra.'

The guys looked slightly disappointed.

'Oh,' said Rookie, 'that same one you had here? You didn't ship it all the way over there, did you?' He nodded to the left as though Wales were on the other side of the bar.

William coughed. 'No, no. It's a more up-to-date model.'

'Brand new, I suppose?' said Boetie more as a statement than a question.

'No, not quite.' Again there was that look of disappointment and William felt he was losing them slightly. 'But near enough,' he added. 'Last year's model.'

They all nodded again, more vigorously this time and seemed to be back on an even keel with him. The rest of the evening, in fact the rest of the holiday had passed superbly. He ate steak every night; he bought the guys drinks at 25p a go; and he even left Nyoni enough money for his son's school fees for a year. William Lloyd left Zimbabwe feeling good about himself.

The next year, he had been as eager to return as the previous. Although he was beginning to feel slightly more settled – he had taken out a long-term lease on a small terraced house – he still had that longing for the familiar, the really familiar, that could only be found in one place. Things were different though, alarmingly different. There was nothing whatsoever to be bought in the shops. Row upon row upon shelf upon shelf was empty, except for the odd cluster of pool chemicals and toilet rolls. There was nothing to eat, nothing at all.

Everyone was very down at heart and couldn't understand why he had come back.

'Why d'you come back here, man? I thought you could travel anywhere. *Sheez like*, if I were you, I'd be out there, man, travelling around, going somewhere *different*.'

He couldn't help but feel a little embarrassed. Saying things like 'It's home' or 'Shit, I've missed this place' would sound a little contrite. More than anything, they would reveal how much a stranger he was. The one thing he didn't want anyone to say was 'Well, you don't live here anymore. You don't know what it's like.'

The bar was virtually deserted. Nyoni cut a rather dejected figure behind the counter. He was jovial, of course, when William came in. There were the usual handshakes and back slaps, but he didn't say very much, except to ask how the UK was and tell Billy how bad things were.

Billy didn't stay with Boetie and his wife this time. He had meant to, it's what he wanted, but Boetie had sounded rather hesitant on the phone. There was an extra-long pause and Billy had the distinct feeling that Boetie was repeating everything that Billy said as if someone else was listening. Boetie didn't say outright that he couldn't come, in fact he said he'd be most welcome, but then he made all these comments like 'But you're gonna have to bring your own food, my boet.' Or 'Do you think you can get a couple of sheep on the plane?'

So Billy had elected to stay at a guest house in Suburbs, which was exceptionally reasonably priced, considering the exchange rate, although the food was not quite as plentiful as he might have hoped.

The next year, Billy didn't go home, nor the next. Truth to tell, he was scared. He had had this feeling, a very distinct feeling, that his friends all thought him a failure. Why else would he keep coming home? He didn't like the way he had felt an outsider, a Pom. He had missed it, of course, but had put his head down and worked his butt off and so two more winters, summers and springs had passed on Mud Island before he decided once more to pack his bags and head for warmer climes.

He was pleased this time to find things a little more upbeat. Rookie had gone to work in Francistown and Frikie and his wife had gone to live with their daughter in Polokwane, but although his friends had dwindled, Billy still felt things were on the up. Nyoni was happy to be earning greenbacks now and everyone was happy that food was back on the shelves. Boetie was considering opening a little restaurant at the club, but he would have to be quick because they were popping up everywhere nowadays – even the Bowling Club had opened a café – and who the heck played bowls these days?

Billy had returned to Wales with a greater sense of contentment than when he had left. Zim was on the up, man. He knew it was too good to go down the drain. They were strong, hey, those guys, but no one was gonna let them go down without a fight.

The following year saw him raring to go again, but finances weren't quite on his side. The recession was moving in and work was not that easy to come by. Billy began to think of returning to Zimbabwe, but for good this time. He looked at his savings and decided he probably had enough to buy himself a small flat somewhere and set himself up in business. It was a dream he liked to consider, although somewhere in the back of his mind that fear of Edith Duly continued to loom. He decided to do another trip out to Zim, a reccy, to see how viable his plans would be.

Boetie was there, of course, somehow he always would be. He fetched Billy from the large hanger that served as Bulawayo's airport now that the old one was no longer in use. He was there in his long socks and short shorts, standing outside smoking one of his forty a day.

Things were not so good, he told Billy on the drive to Bulawayo. *Ja*, sure there was food and stuff, but, hey, there weren't enough greenbacks kicking around.

'Look at this one,' he said, pulling a wad of notes from his top pocket and showing him the top one. 'Old Benj has just about left the building.' The note was old and dirty and extremely faded. 'This is what I call a hot potato. You want to get rid of it as soon as you can.'

Billy grinned. 'I know where I can do that! How things at the bar?'

Boetie shrugged. 'Wouldn't know really. Hardly go there these days.'

Billy's heart sank. 'Why? What's the shupa?'

Boetie shrugged and answered dismissively: 'Dunno. You'll see.'

A couple of days later, Boetie agreed to take him to the club. Billy was inexplicably excited but tried hard not to show it. He adopted the nonchalant attitude of the returning resident who has been doing bigger and better things elsewhere.

The first thing he noticed was the décor. The walls had been repainted a lemony yellow and all the furniture had been replaced with expensive teak bar stools, chairs and coffee tables. The bar now had a menu with things like 'soup de la jour', and 'apres mains'. The bar was crowded with youngsters drinking cocktails out of long, tall glasses and he could hardly hear himself over the music.

Boetie ordered them each a Castle while Billy stood in bewilderment, looking around him for something he recognised. Out of the corner of his eye, he noticed two young girls looking across at him and Boetie and laughing quietly. He picked up a fragment of their conversation – something about his long socks – but he was too shocked to consider it too deeply.

'Nyoni?' he suddenly said, realising another change in the décor; the barman was nowhere to be seen.

'Gone,' said Boetie, taking a slurp of his beer and curling his bottom lip upwards.

'*Where?*' Billy was shocked to his bones.

Boeite shrugged. 'Somewhere else?' he said, facetiously.

'But *where?*' Billy persisted, looking frantically around as though he could spot Nyoni in the crowd somewhere.

Boeitie shrugged again, downed his beer and wiped his hand across his mouth.

'He's gone like so many other people have gone. Only he doesn't keep coming back.' Billy caught a note of – what was it? – irony? in Boetie's voice.

'I love Zimbabwe,' Billy nodded emphatically. 'It's my home.'

'No, it's not,' said Boetie. A quietness had entered his voice, which added a certain strength to his words. 'You live in the UK now – you left.'

Billy didn't know what to say in return – that he wanted to come back? – and instead had let his eyes roam the bar area, taking in the crowds of laughing youngsters, cigarettes balanced jauntily in smiling mouths, beer bottles raised to lips with the confidence that only the young can have. Perhaps Boetie was right; he *had* left and, in doing so, had forfeited his right to want everything to stay the same.

The following year saw Billy once again at the airport, but this time it was Cardiff, not Gatwick. He had decided at last to trace his Scottish roots. After all, if this was going to be his home, he may as well have roots. He had even brought the photograph, the one of the stern, unsmiling woman. As he sat in the bar of the departure lounge, he lifted his beer to his lips and patted the envelope in his left breast pocket.

'Cheers,' he said to himself. 'Scotland here I come, man. Let's hope you're ready for me.'

THE RHYTHM OF LIFE

The day the rains started, Pattie's son died. It was the fifteenth of November. Craig swore they'd start that day. 'Halfway through November' was what he always said; the fifteenth was his chosen date.

'Told you so,' he said, as we sat on the kitchen step and watched the first swollen plops smatter violently on the ground. I rolled my eyes in jest. Then Pattie arrived and told us her son was dead.

'It is better,' said Craig, for Garikayi had been ill for a long time.

'No, it is not better!' she wailed. 'He was my son and now he is dead!' She held her stomach and leaned against the wall. I put my arm around her.

He was buried the next day. I was glad of the rain, of the relief from the heat, until I thought of the funeral. That morning I had given her money and a ten-kilogram packet of mealie meal to help feed the mourners who had gathered. I knew it would not be enough.

In the afternoon, I sat on the verandah reading. Dylan Thomas. How apt was the soft rain falling just beyond the steps, the gurgle of water in the drainpipe, the gentle plash, plash of it onto the grass and nearby pot plants. A wet woody smell rose from the woven grass carpets on the floor, but it was comforting, as was the cool of the cushion behind my back.

Getting up to fetch a glass of water, I caught sight of the hanging baskets Garikayi had made. The fuchsia leant lazily out as the baskets turned slowly in the wet breeze. He had also made the carved wooden elephant that acted as a pot stand near the door. Its trunk was too large so it always gave the impression it was about to fall over, but it never had. Somehow it had always managed to maintain its balance and stand, if not completely upright, at a slightly tilting angle, as though it were about to charge. It was this that gave it an element of unusual dignity. There were other things Garikayi had made: the pots I had my hydrangea in, a rough garden table and a birdbath. He had also established our vegetable garden that now thrived full of beans, butternut, gem squash, spinach, carrots and onions. That was before he became too thin and ill to work, although even then he would turn up at least two days a week and wander slowly round the garden, cutting off a dead flower head here and there, or occasionally poking his finger into the soil as though it would yield something of interest.

'I don't know why he bothers,' Craig said once. He was sitting outside one lunchtime, smoking and blowing blue clouds of bitterness into the air.

'Don't say that,' I said and he looked at me, eyes half closed and laughed, a short cynical 'ha'. I turned away and felt my stomach contract.

The last few times we saw Garikayi, he just sat and stared. That was in September and now he was dead.

It rained all through December and January and the garden flourished. One day in February, Pattie came to work with her arms full of St. Joseph Lilies. They grew under the blue gums along the railway line, hundreds of bobbing white bonnets, like a crowd of excited debutantes, whispering and giggling before their first dance.

I filled two vases and still had more left over. She started to bring them twice a week and I had to give them away. I couldn't bring myself to ask her to stop. Garikayi used to bring them before, though never as many. It was as though our smiled thanks and expressions of delight were really an acknowledgement of him and she needed him to live on.

In the autumn, we planted sweet peas. I was afraid that the frost of the approaching winter might kill them off, but it didn't. By June, they were already pushing their way upwards and, in August, they were halfway up the trellis we had tied them to.

The warm, dry wind of August blew the flames of veldt fires through the bush. One reached our back garden. Craig ranted, but there was nothing we could do. We stood ready with buckets of water should the fire come any closer, but it didn't. Garikayi's vegetable garden remained untouched.

By October, Craig and I had our bet going again. He still swore by the fifteenth of November, but he was wrong this time. The rains came on the seventeenth.

'Near enough,' he said, not looking me in the eye.

Pattie had a day off. She went to her son's graveside for the last time.

'No more,' she said when she returned. 'He is not there anymore.'

I knew what she meant. We didn't go back anymore either. There was a time when we'd take a drive out Headlands way. We'd go as far as the turnoff to the farm and pull over. Sometimes it felt as though we were going home, as though we'd just gone shopping for the day. I'd imagine what we'd have bought, what I was going to make for dinner, what had happened while we'd been away. After a while, we gave up and sometimes I felt we had always lived in town and never known any other life.

We began to look forward: next year there'd be more St. Joseph Lilies, more sweet peas to plant, more fires to put out. It is perhaps to our detriment that we rely so heavily on the soft, undulating rhythm of life for our sense of security and continuity. How many have done so only to have their plans changed, their lives cut short, their hopes curtailed? But what is there without that hope of the future, the reassurance of stability? Do we not all rage against the dying of the light?

'In April, we plant poppies,' said Pattie, not long after Christmas. She was looking in a notebook of Garikayi's, his carefully made notes of seasonal plants.

'Yes, I think we shall,' I said and she nodded and put the notebook away with a sigh.

I didn't see the poppies or the sweet peas that year. In April we left. The house was sold and we waved Zimbabwe good-bye. I miss it often. Most of all, I miss the way the seasons change, the way the sun slants on the late afternoon lawn, the half-light of dawn. No one brings me St. Joseph Lilies and we have no space for a vegetable garden. I do, however, have Garikayi's notebook, pressed into my hands by a tearful Pattie. I flick through it sometimes when I am most homesick. I think of what Pattie will be growing, how the vegetable garden is doing and whether the sweet peas will survive the frost.

Lately, I have taken to carrying the notebook in my handbag. I hold it close as I squash into overfilled railway

137

carriages, as I shudder and shake on the long journey to work and back. It beats out the rhythm of home and I find comfort, still.

THESE I HAVE LOVED

It was that particular time of the afternoon when the world is bathed in a golden hush; the time when babies sleep in prams under large, shady trees and dogs flop on cold concrete floors; the time when the lavender, the delphiniums, the petunias and the antirrhinums – there are so many – with half closed eyes turn their faces against the sun and doze; when the heat rises in a hazy stupor that spreads outwards and upwards and even the insects move in a slow, haphazard way as though fighting the desire to stop and sleep.

Shirley sat in a cool corner of the verandah and sipped her tea. Her glasses lay on a small table beside her next to her overturned book. She glanced at her watch; in another twenty minutes it would be three o'clock. She still adhered to the colonial instruction that the sun should be avoided between the hours of one and three. It was one she felt had served her well in her life and she had no intention of throwing it aside in her later years. Not like her son and his English wife who had got into the car just after lunch and departed, their long, unhappy faces drawing into the distance as the car reversed. They had piled swimming costumes and towels and a bottle of sun cream into a basket – *Don't forget hats!* – and gone in search of a pool. English girls are so different, thought Shirley, as she watched the girl get into the car with her long legs and her denim shorts and the oversized hat. It wasn't that one didn't like them, it was just that one wished they weren't quite so difficult to please when they came to Africa. Only just that morning when Shirley had poured the girl a glass of water, she had held it up to the light for inspection. And the mosquitoes. One never heard the end of mosquitoes.

Shirley was surprised they had left the baby with her. She had seen the girl's mouth quiver with uncertainty, noticed the way the child was handed over, with a tightening of the touch, an apologetic kiss. We won't be long, her son had said to her, but the words were really meant for his wife.

But she'll be safe with me, she thought. Safe in the shade of the garden, in the fuzz of sleep. And so she had been. Shirley had put her where she had put all her babies, in a soft glade, protected by a frangipani and a hedge of dusty pink bougainvillea. She had not seen the baby so contented since her son and his little family had arrived. She watched it for a while, fascinated by the gentle smile, the way the little body relaxed. Like a figure on the beach might watch a swimmer leave the shore, stretching further and further into the ocean, so she watched it push away and find itself afloat on a beautiful warm sea of sleep.

A person walked slowly round the side of the house, a slight hesitancy in her walk as though she were barefoot and picking her way across a field of thorns. It was Elizabeth, out of her uniform now and wearing instead a long, pleated skirt with a shirt in matching navy. She carried a brown leather handbag that Shirley had given her and an umbrella that she would open up once out on the road to shield her from the sun. A small brown hat perched on her head.

In her mind's eye, Shirley followed Elizabeth down the hot,

blue road. She saw her stop at the corner to push the umbrella up and out, saw it burst into a pattern of white daisies on a black background, saw it poised on her shoulder, felt the heat flicker against the surface, the sudden shadow that bloomed behind her head.

Elizabeth would be going to see her grandson in the hospital, as she did every Saturday. The poor boy with the twisted brain who lay on frayed white sheets and shouted at the sunbeams. Elizabeth never gave up. She took him fried beans and a container of porridge, which he sometimes threw at the wall and sometimes at her.

Shirley knew where Elizabeth would stand to get the bus, how she would adjust her hat a little to the right just before getting on, how she would sit upright, looking straight ahead as though the long road that wound down the hill into town and past the hospital was one long meandering ribbon that some child in its playfulness had begun to unfurl, letting it run and run – and had then tossed it in the air, attempted to catch it and stumbled, and then, losing interest, let it fall somewhere between houses and buildings and someone's name on a street sign – a revolutionary, a fighter, a madman, a dictator. But if you followed it, if you could just keep going, you'd reach fields and rivers and homesteads, and beyond that the forests and the mountains and the sea that rolled in, the white waves kissing the beach in delight. Beyond that even, the universe, the planets, a hundred million galaxies of stars.

But Elizabeth would have no idea of that. For her, the road ended at the edge of town where it tapered into the nothingness of the creamy brown grass.

The tin roof creaked and a fly buzzed in circles on the low

wall of the verandah. Shirley took a sip of her tea; it was black, but the lemon lifted the taste and took the edge off the bitterness. She was aware of someone in the garden. It was Sam working overtime, cutting back the bougainvillea. Sam, dear old Sam! How long had he been with her now? Was it nineteen or twenty years?

She liked to watch him work for he moved about the garden with ease, turning over the soil with his little trowel, breaking the soft dark clods, his fingers making warm beds for the new seedlings. He was wearing a new pair of blue overalls that she had recently bought him and a green hat that he pulled down over his eyes. She was always comforted by the sight of him for he knew the garden and he worked without instruction. There had been a time, during a visit to her son in England, when this had bothered her. She hadn't liked to think that the garden was entirely in someone else's hands and she made sure to give him a long list of things he needed to do. The paths, for instance, must be carefully maintained and the hedges cut back after the rains. It was the attention to detail that many people often forgot, but not Sam. No, not Sam.

She had returned to find everything in order and found that it saddened her, so she had made sure to move a few pots and mention that the hanging baskets weren't getting enough sun. Sam, of course, followed her every instruction without question. Now she watched as he trimmed the border around the trees and along the concrete path to the fishpond.

She was filled then with a strange kind of love, not for people, but for the place. She wanted to stand up and reach out her arms to the garden. She wanted to run down the steps as she had as a child and onto the grass; she wanted to enter the cool green places she had known, the place under the frangipani, the cove of darkness under the bougainvillea. She wanted to sink into the damp soil and feel her roots begin to shoot and grow. She wanted to feel the orgasmic joy of expansion as she pushed her way to the top of the soil, bursting through, unbending her small green head, growing upwards and outwards, sprouting leaves and buds and flowers and seeds. She wanted her arms to be picked up by the breeze, to feel a shiver as the cool water from the can trickled down her back, the touch of a hand. The gasp of joy.

It was ten minutes to three.

Her father slept in a chair next to her, his legs stretched out in front of him and a hat pulled down over his eyes. The tea on a small table next to him would grow cold, she knew, but she was hesitant to disrupt this ritual. Saturday afternoon, after a light lunch, she liked to sit with her father on the verandah and watch the afternoon unfold. Their roles had changed somewhat since the days when her parents would take their tea after lunch, sitting straight-backed on the cane chairs.

Instinctively, Shirley's eyes turned to a light pink gardenia at the end of the flower bed. Under it were her mother's ashes. It was blooming, she was happy to see. She liked to think of it as some sort of message, some sign that her mother was still with them.

Perfection.

She felt her eyes close gently in the golden warmth of the afternoon. She tilted her head back so that all she could see through her half-closed eyelids was the hot white gleam of the concrete steps leading up to the verandah. A dove called gently, the somnolent sound of afternoons in Africa. A fly buzzed and her father began to snore.

Something, perhaps the sudden silence that descended just as she felt herself slip into oblivion, made her sit up. Startled, she looked over at her father who was still fast asleep, a silver line of dribble edging its way down the corner of his mouth. Sam piled spiky branches of bougainvillea onto his wheelbarrow and pushed it away down the path to the compost heap at the back of the garden. It seemed as if the world itself had just shivered.

Don't let her sleep too long. Wake her up, please. We want her to sleep tonight.

Shirley closed her eyes again but could not sleep. She thought of the girl, the English girl with her large hat and her sunscreen. She thought of the way she had held the glass of water up to the light. The previous evening, she had tried so hard to engage her in conversation over dinner.

'If you were here in June,' she had said, 'you wouldn't believe how cold Zimbabwe can get.'

But there had been little response beyond a perfunctory raised eyebrow. Now, she thought to herself, she will never be here in June. She will only come as a tourist in the hot summer months and complain about the heat and the mosquitoes.

She had a sudden feeling of panic, not a gentle, fluttering feeling, but something much sharper and enclosing. The fear was not within her, but outside: it blanketed the house and garden in a fine, grey shadow. She pulled herself straighter in her chair and reached for her tea; it was still there. Everything was the same, wasn't it? Sam's bent head, the baby, the dahlias, the gardenia.

It was she who was missing. The house, it was empty. Leaves blew across the garden. They only kept Sam on two days a week now; it was just enough to keep everything green, but not long enough to keep it tidy.

Her son arrived in one car and another followed from which a young couple emerged. They looked at the garden and nodded their heads at each other.

'Beautiful. I'm not much of a gardener myself,' laughed the woman.

'You don't need to be. Keep Sam on and he'll run the show for you.'

Her son carried a bunch of keys. He unlocked the house and led the couple through: this is the kitchen and next door is the dining room. If we were staying on, I'd probably knock them into one. This is the bathroom and this is the smallest bedroom. A long pause. This is the master bedroom. It was my mother's.

It was my mother's. It was my mother's. Shirley stood up and walked to the edge of the verandah.

A splattering of shadows now lay across the path as though someone had stumbled and spilled a bucket of them. The shade the baby was asleep in had deepened and grown. It was like a tide coming in and the pram was a tiny boat washed further and further out to sea.

'Sam, Sam! Not so much.' Sam turned with a start as though something had stung him. She hadn't meant to shout so loudly. The baby stirred. 'You'll cut that bush back so much, there will be nothing left of it soon.'

The baby cried more insistently.

Shirley lifted the baby out of his pram and rocked him gently.

'Ssh, shh,' she whispered, placing him on her shoulder and gently rubbing his back. 'Did I wake you? I'm sorry. You were having a lovely sleep, weren't you?'

When he had quietened, she touched his head with her lips.

'Come with me and see my garden,' she said. 'Let me show you all the things I love.' She walked along the path, noting how clipped and neat the grass was. She flicked on the switch in the box at the side of the miniature fountain. The water gurgled through the top of the statue of the little boy. She imagined him squealing with delight, even though the water was initially hot. She looked at the baby whose eyes were closing again.

At the fishpond, she stood and stared into its depths. She usually liked to imagine it went on and on, dark and cool and mysterious. This time, the presence of three large goldfish darting under the lily pads comforted her. She knew that if she stepped in, the water wouldn't even reach her thigh. She knew that she could walk across it in three large bounds.

'Look, fish,' she said, pointing with her one free hand. 'Big orange fish.'

Sam turned the spray on.

'Make sure you keep it in the shade,' she cautioned him. He nodded politely. Of course, the spray was already in the shade.

The baby was asleep again. She lowered him gently back into his pram and covered him with the mosquito net. She tried to imagine him as an old man sitting on a verandah, looking out over his garden. There were years and years to come; millions of moments to live. If this was his one and only visit here, if he were to never ever come back, would he remember it? Of course not, she smiled. But somewhere she wanted him to remember the afternoon, to remember lying on his back and staring at the square of blue above him as the shade stretched over him and lulled him to sleep.

It did not seem that long ago that she was a child playing in the corner of the garden; excited when she heard the car door slam and herald her father's arrival back home for lunch; running up the verandah steps when her mother called her to wash her hands.

She fetched her pair of garden scissors and cut long sprays of carnations and chrysanthemums. They would look lovely in a vase on the dinner table. She paused. She would cut some for the bedrooms as well. For her son and his wife with her oversized hat.

The birthdays and Christmases, the weddings and funerals, the betrothals and the secret trysts and the broken hearts: all the events that make up a life. She was at once a little girl hiding in the dappled sunlight behind the hedge, hoping not to be found, and a middle-aged woman with a bunch of flowers.

Behind her, her father stirred. She turned and smiled.

'We'll leave the baby sleep a little longer,' she said. 'They need all the rest they can get at this age. Come, I'll make some fresh tea. I am sure yours has gone cold.'

THE FOUNTAIN OF LETHE

'I notice you've cut down the trees,' Julia said to the receptionist as she filled in the forms. She tried to disguise the accusatory tone in her voice, smiling brightly as she wrote down her details: name, address, telephone number. It had been a disappointment on arrival to find the hotel perched alone on the hill with not a tree near it. The closest plantation was at least a forty-five-minute walk away. Only the last fifty metres of the road leading up to the hotel were still lined with massive eucalyptus. Yet still she had felt a flutter of excitement as she had driven up to the door. They were back.

The receptionist was a young woman of about twenty, who couldn't possibly have been working there long.

'The trees,' Julia repeated. 'Pine trees. They used to grow very close to the hotel. I used to come here as a child. With my parents,' she added. 'We used to go walking through the forest.' She weaved her hand through the air in a gentle snaking action.

The receptionist smiled politely and then turned back to her computer. 'Rooms 9 and 14,' she said. 'Do you need someone to help you carry your luggage?'

'9 and 14? I asked for adjoining rooms.'

The receptionist scanned her computer screen. 'You asked for two twin rooms.'

'Yes, adjoining each other.'

'I'm sorry, but we don't have adjoining twin rooms. Our adjoining rooms are double and single.'

'They didn't used to be. They were always twin rooms.'

The receptionist shrugged her shoulders and drew in her lips in an apologetic smile.

'All right. I'll take a double and a single. My daughter can sleep with me.'

'I'm sorry, but they're booked.'

Julia's heart sank. She leaned closer to the counter and dropped her voice. 'It's my dad, you see.' She motioned over her shoulder to where her father sat on a chair by the wall. 'He... he... well, he wanders off. Sometimes. When he's in a different place.' She watched the receptionist's face, hoping the gravity of what she was saying would sink in without the need for further explanation.

'He'll be on the same floor.'

She pulled herself straight. 'It doesn't matter. I *need* to be near him.'

She felt the receptionist's eyes flicker over her and onto her father. Rosie, her nine-year-old daughter, slumped in the chair next to him, her head on her backpack and one arm around her teddy.

'Could you bear with us for tonight?' asked the receptionist in a low monotone that irritated her. *Bear with us.* Julia hated the forced politeness and lack of any initiative on the part of the young woman. If it wasn't on the computer, it couldn't happen. 'Perhaps I can move you tomorrow.'

She thought. Dad was tired; he'd probably just go to sleep. She could lock the door, although she hated doing that sort of thing. He wasn't mad, he just got confused. He clung to familiarity like a shipwrecked sailor hanging onto a piece of floating debris – except that when he got to dry ground, he refused to let go, not realising that the very thing that had kept him afloat was now a dead weight, holding him down.

'All right,' she conceded. 'I'll take those rooms. We need to get changed for dinner.'

'The kitchen closes in half an hour,' said the receptionist, looking up at the clock on the wall.

'Half an hour? It's only eight o'clock.'

'Yes, the dining room closes at nine. Last orders from the kitchen are at half-past eight.'

Julia let out a sigh of frustration and her handbag fell off her shoulder. She pulled the strap up clumsily, ruching the sleeve of her shirt. 'Could you ask them to wait? We've driven a long way today. We're all tired.'

The receptionist shook her head with a weak smile. It was the perfunctory apology of a schoolgirl who hasn't done her homework.

They didn't make it to the dining room that night. Julia had taken her father to his room, laid out some clean clothes for him to wear, and run a sink full of warm water so that he could wash his face before dinner. Then she had gone to her own room and done the same for Rosie, who had perked up and was trying the different channels on the television after examining the contents of the mini bar. By the time she went back to check on her father, he was fast asleep on top of the bed, the clean set of clothes pushed into a tangle under his feet. When she attempted to wake him, he raised his shoulder against her petulantly, turning his head into the pillow. She slipped off his shoes and covered him with a blanket from the spare bed.

Back in her room, she found Rosie happily ensconced in bed, watching cartoons and eating the complimentary mint chocolates.

'These were on the pillows.' She held up a chocolatey mess in one hand and, in the other, an untouched sweet wrapped in green-and-white spotted silver paper.

'I think one's for me,' Julia said.

'Oh,' said Rosie, looking from one hand to another. 'I think I ate yours. Sorry.'

Julia picked up the room service menu and ran her eyes over the choices. Hamburgers or chicken burgers. Everything with chips.

Julia picked up the phone and began to dial. 'I'll order you a burger.'

'OK.' Rosie settled herself back onto the large, puffy pillows and flicked channels.

But the phone didn't work. Julia tried unplugging it both at the wall and on the handset, but nothing helped. She looked at her watch. The kitchen would be closing soon anyway. She doubted it stayed open for room service orders.

She searched through the large bag in which she had packed a picnic lunch for the journey. Two sandwiches and an apple remained. She offered them to Rosie first.

'There's only cheese.'

'I don't like cheese.'

'Have an apple, then. I'm going to have a shower. If you change your mind, take a sandwich.'

When Julia emerged from the bathroom ten minutes later,

Rosie was asleep, the remote in her hand and the apple untouched. Julia gently eased her into bed, switched off the main light, leaving only the bedside lamp on, and sat on a chair. A wave of loneliness surprised her. What was it, that particular feel of hotel rooms? That mixture of holiday excitement and disappointment that one wavered between.

She towel-dried her hair and ran a comb through it. A plastic-covered brochure on the desk detailed all the activities available at the hotel: swimming, squash, tennis, birdwatching and horse-riding. The latter had been scratched out with a biro. A separate piece of paper advertised the services of a spa. A sentence in block capitals announced that prices were subject to fluctuation.

It was an automatic reaction to reach for her phone in her bag. She remembered it wasn't there, and drew her hand back. No phones. No laptops. No computer games. Nothing they wouldn't have had in 1985. *Good old-fashioned fun.* She would have liked to have sent Nicola some photos: the view from the terrace, the path through the trees, the imposing entrance to the hotel. She wanted to say, *Hey, look! I'm back here.*

You're going there? You're brave.

Nicola's words.

All those hills.

As it was, the Wi-Fi, one of the few additions to the hotel, was useless to her. She fluffed up the pillows on her side of the bed and settled down with the remote, quickly putting the sound on mute in case it woke Rosie. Three grainy channels offered the news, a football match between Juventus and Milan, and a movie she had seen before, but couldn't remember the name of. She watched with little interest as

Harrison Ford broke out of jail and jumped over walls with a broken arm. She watched his lips move in American English. God damn you. She heard that much at least.

Tired, but knowing she would find it difficult to sleep, she sank further into the pillows and looked around the room: at the heavy, dull counterpane; the Bible by the side of the bed, courtesy of the Gideons; the curtains, which she hadn't bothered to close because of all the white flouncy stuff that blocked out the night. Perhaps she should have brought her phone after all. She could have hidden it in her suitcase to prevent any protest from Rosie and taken it out at moments like these. She could have messaged Rob to let them know they had arrived safely. *No news is good news.* Isn't that what she had said?

Rob said she was foolish to drive to Nyanga that way, but then he had been against the trip from the start.

'Take the road to Zvishivane,' he said. 'Then carry on to Masvingo and Birchenough Bridge. Mutare isn't too far from there.'

'That's easier if you are going to the Vumba. If I went that way, I'd still need to drive through Mutare and on to Nyanga.'

'Still faster than through Harare. All that traffic adds at least another hour and a half onto a journey.'

But she was determined. She avoided Rob's raised eyebrows and that look that said 'heed my words', and talked excitedly about the road trip ahead.

Abba. They had to take Abba. And Bruce Springsteen and Chris de Burgh and Roger Whittaker. Tapes would have been good, but they could no longer be played in the car. Instead, she downloaded five hours of music and dug out a few CD compilations – *Hits of the 70s and 80s*, and *The Complete Leo Sayer*.

'Good luck,' Rob had said to Rosie that morning as he disentangled her from the seat belt she had been trying to put round both her and her teddy. 'You're going to need it.'

'Nothing wrong with a bit of 80s music,' Julia retorted.

'No, nothing at all. For the first hundred kilometres. You may want some variation after that.' He ruffled Rosie's hair, gave her a high five and closed the door.

'Nicola always maintains we were psychologically damaged by the amount of Abba we listened to on family holidays,' she laughed, switching the engine on and searching for a particular song on her phone.

'I rest my case.'

'"Dancing Queen". What better way to start. Remember this, Dad?'

Rob glanced over at her father in the passenger seat.

The old man hadn't wanted to go.

'We're off to Nyanga, Dad.'

'Never heard of the place.'

'Yes, you have. You'll see.'

'Rubbish.'

'You used to love it. You and Mom. We used to go every August holidays. We loved the walks through the forest—'

'Don't believe a word of it. Not a word.'

'We'll have a great time. Dad, please Dad.'

Dad, please Dad.

She swept up the pieces of green-and-white spotted foil that Rosie had left in a small heap on the bed, remembering the way her mother always had mints in her bag and how, on long car trips, when she and Nicola were getting fractious, she'd dig around and bring them out.

Let's see what we have in here, girls.

Another wave of loneliness washed up from inside.

Mint imperials. That's what they were called. Little rounds of white that smelt of the cool depths of Mom's bag: hand cream and cigarettes and folded letters; an address book and a diary with a dark blue cover and an elastic band wrapped round it. A lipstick – Queen of the Nile – a nail file and an errant curler. School photographs with our fringes cut too short and our hair pulled back so tightly, it made our eyes water.

You can't make her come back.

Rob's words.

I know that. It's just… if I could stir some memory. If I could rekindle the *feeling*.

Perhaps he doesn't want to remember.

More of Rob's words.

He might not remember her, but he might remember being happy.

Who's it for, Jules? You or him?

For him. Everything I do is for him.

What about you? Have you come to terms with your mother's death yet?

Come to terms. Come to terms. The words floated above her, but she didn't reach out to them. Instead, she switched channels to what was now a wrestling match. She winced as a man with long silver hair and a red bandana was jumped on from the side of the ring by an equally large man in what looked like a tight black swimming costume.

After dinner, we run back to the room, knowing what awaits. We slip the key in the lock, we twist the door handle, and step inside. The heavy counterpanes have been removed. The top sheet and blanket are pulled down, and there on each pillow is a circle of shiny green. It is as though fairies have come while we were out.

We eat them too quickly. The chocolate is sweet. It sticks in our throats and makes us cough.

Now the fight.

Mom, can we have yours?

Please.

Please.

She smiles. Her hand hovers between us.

Why doesn't one of you have it today and one of you tomorrow?

That's not fair.

Of course it's fair.

Dad pops his chocolate in his mouth. He lies on top of the bed wearing only his shorts, reading Time *magazine and watching the news on ZBC.*

Mom searches her bag for a second-place-end-of-the-meal complimentary mint to assuage the feelings of the loser. Usually me.

Dad switches off the news. In our adjoining room, Nicola and I lie in our beds deciding who can have the notepaper and envelopes.

I take the room service menu and Nicola takes a list of important phone numbers. Tomorrow, Mom will tell us that these are not complimentary and we have to put them back.

We decide that we can each have a bar of soap from the bathroom, knowing we'll be given more tomorrow if we make it look like we have used it all up. After more argument, this time in loud, hard whispers, Nicola gets a shower cap and I settle on a bag that says Sanitary Towels Only on it.

Rosie was up early, doing handstands on the bed so that she could roll over into the comfort of the pillows. Julia went to check on her father, who was still asleep. In the dining room, Rosie piled a bowl high with cornflakes, Coco Pops and tinned grapefruit pieces. Then she eagerly awaited a full English breakfast while trying out different types of fruit juice. Heartened by her daughter's appetite, Julia approached her own breakfast with more gusto than she felt. A knot of apprehension twisted deep in her stomach.

The dining room hadn't changed that much. A coat of paint, perhaps, and different colour chairbacks, but little else. It was emptier than she remembered, and the buffet not quite as vast in range. She noticed the waiter's eyes following Rosie nervously as she went for her third glass of juice.

At breakfast, lunch and supper we look for our favourite waiter, Jethro. He knows our names and asks us about school. We ask him about his wife and his children. He is as familiar as a piece of furniture, with a smile like a sunbeam.

'How long are we staying?' asked Rosie.

'The weekend. Why?'

'No reason. Just asking.'

'Let's go for a walk,' Julia said. 'While it's still cool. Gumpy won't be up for a while.'

We start early after breakfast, when our stomachs are full of scrambled egg, bacon, tomato and sausage.

'Should keep us going,' says Dad as he pushes his wide-

*brimmed blue hat on and slings a small satchel over his shoulder.
'Onwards and upwards.'*

*We follow the road through the forest, feeling the pull of our
bodies as it winds further down, down, down into the valley.*

She didn't plan to be gone long. Just a short walk down the
drive to the road and maybe back up through the scrubby bush
at the front of the hotel where the pine forest used to be. The
path was bound to still be in use. Then they could get Dad up
and give him his breakfast. She changed her mind when they
got to the top of the drive. It was unlikely that they would
encounter many cars; the hotel was ten kilometres off the main
road for a start, at the end of a narrow dusty strip of dirt that
dropped into a valley and then rose sharply again. It was
situated on a smudge of green on an otherwise grey-blue hill,
surrounded by other, larger hills, upon which pine tree after
pine tree grew, like soldiers lined up for battle. She had a
memory of the trees surrounding the hotel itself, of walking
through a densely wooded area, heavy with the smell of
crushed pine needles and the warm wet of decay.

She opted to walk through the sparse vegetation made up
of straggly pine saplings and occasional thickets of dry
bracken. Rosie was subdued as they set off, and clung to her
hand, which did not make walking easy. She didn't shake it off
though, or encourage the girl to walk on her own. She also
had a need to hold someone's hand.

'Smell the air, Rosie,' she said. 'Can you smell it?'

Rosie sniffed in an exaggerated dog-like manner. 'No.'

'Pine. That lovely fresh smell.'

'Oh.'

It was the smell of holidays, of freedom. The smell of walks and woodsmoke and time that unravelled in soft waves behind you as you meandered through the trees.

Beat you to the road!

Last one there is a rotten egg!

'All this used to be trees,' she said to Rosie, sweeping her hand across the denuded landscape. 'Lots and lots of trees. Aunty Nicola and I used to call it the Enchanted Forest.'

'Why did they cut them down?'

'I'm not sure. There must have been a fire,' she said, noting the blackened stumps. 'Look, this is the original path. Now imagine this is all full of really tall pine trees.'

Rosie looked around and then, with decided resignation, she set off, skipping. Julia felt her heart lift in response.

'We used to imagine we would find fairies here and pixies. Elves, all sorts of magical creatures.'

Without answering, Rosie continued to hop along the path.

'We stopped coming here when I was twelve,' Julia called after her, not really knowing why. 'The road got washed away in the rains and the hotel was closed for months while a bridge was built.'

Mom says we won't be going there again these holidays. There's been a storm. Nicola and I are aghast, but Mom says we'll have fun at home. We can swim at the club and go horse-riding at Aunty Stella's farm. You'll still have a good time, she says. You'll see.

Julia glanced at her watch. Another ten minutes, maybe. Dad always slept late. The heat rose. There was no shade to protect them from the rough glare of the sun and the back of her neck was warm. She wished she had been better prepared and brought more water. Rosie was already most of the way through a bottle. Going downhill was easy. The climb up would almost certainly knock them. She decided not to go as far as the road.

'Can we stop?' Rosie asked.

'Just now. I just want to get to the Fairy Circle. It's where we used to stop and have a break.'

Soon they were near the bottom of the hill. Julia remembered a longer walk filled with trees and birds and squirrels. Where they used to stop in a cool copse and rest on the pine needles was now a dull open area bereft of life. An old Coke can glinted in the sun and flies thronged over a steaming pile of human excrement. She was glad neither of her parents were there.

You're going there. You're brave.

That was why Nicola did not come. Nicola who lived in Canada, who did not come home, except for funerals.

They moved away and found some tree stumps to sit on. The ground was hard and dry; a brittle shaft of grass poked into Julia's ankle, making her cry out.

Rosie looked around at the scrubby bushes and the withered ferns. 'I don't think there's anything here now,' she said. 'You know, elves and things.'

'No, no. You're right. Not now.'

They sat in silence a little longer.

'Perhaps you can swim when we get back,' suggested Julia.

'The pool's closed. Didn't you see the notice?'

'No, no I didn't.'

Rosie picked up a pebble and threw it at a tree stump. It ricocheted back to her feet.

'I'll show you a nice place where Aunty Nicola and I used to hide by the squash court.'

'Yep?'

'It's lovely. A *huge* fig tree and so easy to climb. We used to hide up there and then jump down and scare people.'

She laughed, but Rosie didn't.

'Shall we go back?'

Rosie looked up the hill, her shoulders slumped forward. Her face was blotched red. 'OK,' she said, her resignation obvious. She picked up a stick.

Julia felt a sudden pang of guilt. 'Tell you what, you can have a milkshake when we get back.'

'Do they do milkshakes? They don't look like a milkshake place.'

'Do they do milkshakes? Do they do milkshakes? Of course they do! The best chocolate milkshakes for miles around. Made with fresh farm milk.'

Rosie wasn't convinced. 'Maybe when you were young.'

'Come on,' said Julia. 'Onwards and upwards, as Gumpy would say.'

Where's Mom?

I look behind me. Mom is always at the back. It's our last day, our last walk.

Mom's not coming, says Dad.

And then, before I can ask why: Mom's tired. She needs a break from you two. Come on! Stop daydreaming. Onwards and…

Upwards, we chorus.

As they trudged up the hill and the hotel came in sight, Julia noticed that there were two distinct parts to it. There was the original low, white one-storey building, characteristic of many of the early hotels, which encompassed the reception, the dining room and the lounge; and a newer block of rooms on two levels, built around the late 1950s. She could see how it had developed out of a lonely stopover for the first colonials into a moderately well-run establishment, appealing to those of moderate incomes and moderate aspirations.

A lonely stopover. Is that what it had been to them? Two images came to mind: Mom with her hair in curlers sitting on the verandah outside the room, reading *Fair Lady*. The smell of cigarette smoke, Berkeley extra mild, spiralling above her mother's head. Dad back from a round of golf, sitting at the hotel bar, drinking a cold Castle, talking to whomever was near. 'Scram,' he said when he saw them at the window, looking in. 'Go and play.'

'One, two, three! Coming ready or not!'

I climb further into the thick green of the tree. The sunlight flickers through the cool shadows.

The nearer they got to the hotel, the more she felt a dark wisp of fear rise up from somewhere inside of her. She began to walk faster, trying not to look worried or afraid. Dad. She looked at her watch. Was that how long they had been away? Theirs had been a long journey. Surely he would still be asleep? She felt guilty, negligent. He wouldn't know where he was. He would come and look for her.

The smell of the tree. The feel of the large, shiny leaves against my face. Sweet and cold. If I could just draw them back; if I could just part them. But I don't want to be seen. I can't be seen.

She grabbed Rosie's hand. The girl glanced at her, surprised by the quick jerk of her mother's arm. They walked faster.

Why had they stopped coming?

He wouldn't have gone anywhere, would he? He wasn't interested in anything. He just wanted to be left alone.

What else? What else does she remember?

The path seemed to disappear. A clearing that opened between two bushes led nowhere. A strip of white sand meandered through stunted trees, but ended soon after. Why had they changed everything? Why hadn't it stayed the same?

There were voices. Dad's voice and that of another man. Could I look now? Would the branch creak? What if I drew my foot up? What if I turned just a little to the right?

They began to run. The sun was high in the sky now, and she wished she hadn't worn a long-sleeved top. Black-jacks stuck to the bottoms of her trousers, but she didn't want to stop. The hill seemed to grow steeper and steeper in front of them. If he had wandered off, would anyone try to stop him? There were the stream and the waterfall at the back of the hotel on the other side of the hill. What if he slipped?

They stopped running. They had reached the hotel garden and stood with their hands on their hips, trying to regain their breath. Julia struggled to calm herself, her throat contracting in a pain that extended into her chest, her ribs. It reminded her of another time, another pain.

Rosie started crying, but Julia pulled her along. Up the stairs, along the passage.

You're going back. You're brave.

There is a fumbling sound, like someone undoing a belt. Then another sound. Soft, like mumbling, but getting louder. A deep moan, like someone in pain.

Unlock. The door wouldn't budge, wouldn't open.

'Dad!' She pounded her fists on the door. 'Dad, can you hear me?'

The leaves part. The world below shivers in shadows of green.
'Dad!'
'Dad!'
I smell cigarettes, Madison, for which there is no extra mild. He takes me by the collar and slams me against the wall. What did you see? For God's sake, tell me what you saw. Nothing. Nothing, I promise. A light flickers somewhere in his eyes. He lets go and I slump against the wall, holding my throat. I am sorry, he says. I am sorry.

'Dad, I'm sorry. I left you too long.'

Dad sat on a chair looking out of the window. He turned his milky eyes towards her, and then back at a spot in front of him.

All that could be heard was Rosie's soft sobbing.

'I'm sorry. We'll get a milkshake.'

She shook her head, wiping her tears with the back of her hand. 'I want to go home. I don't like it here.'

Julia knelt by the little girl and took her hands in hers.

'I'm sorry, Rosie. I'm sorry. It's my fault. I just panicked. Everything is okay.'

Rosie nodded.

'Dad?'

He was crying, too. Soft, slow tears made their way down his cheeks. She took out a handkerchief and wiped his face.

That night, Mom puts on too much make up. Her cheeks are red with lashes of blush, and her eyes purple and blue like two swollen bruises. They twitch nervously.

She drinks too much, and talks too loud in a bright, sad way. Jethro avoids us, but she keeps calling him over. He is tired. Unhappy. She sends the fish back three times for being in various

164

states of cooked, none of which suits her. She lights a cigarette. Nicola waves the smoke away with her hand, but there is no stopping her.

Later, Dad closes the interconnecting doors between the two rooms, and Nicola and I lie in silence.

I hope we never come here again, says Nicola.

I think of the pool, the pink soap in the ladies' bathroom, the soft glade of trees at the back of the kitchen, the walk through the pine forest, how the trees reach out to touch you. An enchanted forest. I think of the dark warmth of the tree at the back of the squash courts. I think if I can climb higher, higher, higher...

I hope so, too, I say. But in the dark I cross my fingers.

Eventually, she got through.

'Hello?' It was Rob's voice. 'Ah, the landline. How are the 1980s?'

'We're coming home. It's not the same... a bit run-down if the truth be told.'

'I see.'

'And Dad – he needs familiarity. He... well, he likes what he has chosen to remember.'

It's an apology of sorts.

She puts the phone down.

It will do for now.

MUSIC FROM A FARTHER ROOM

The afternoon hangs suspended in the drowsy heat of late October. The house is quiet with the softness of sleepers. It breathes in and out, gently; the sleepers are drunk with heat and tiredness soon overcame them. The tin roof creaks and a thick triangle of yellow sunlight cuts across the red verandah floor. A lizard tiptoes up the wall, lifts his head and ponders the view from his great height. Somewhere in the distance, a woodpecker sounds twice; a grey lourie plunges noisily into the top branches of a syringa and the lizard scuttles under the eaves of the verandah roof.

It is an old house, it has felt many things: heat and storms and the cold bite of winter. It remains solid, immovable, as it spreads its tentacles of flower beds, palms, pots, a long green lawn, vegetables and herbs; a wheelbarrow, even. At night, it lies open to the dark and winks at the owls, the stars, the night wind, all who come to look for the original brown bush it was built on. And it laughs.

There is a movement from inside the house. There is a slow creak of the wooden floor and two figures appear at the doorway. One is a nurse. She is large and efficient-looking. Her wide, open face is smooth and wrinkle-free. There is the slightest gleam of sweat at her temples, her uniform stretches a little too tightly over her expansive bosom and her wide stockinged feet look uncomfortable in narrow black shoes. Her ankles are slightly swollen; her breath as she helps the old lady, stick thin as she is, into a chair, comes a little fast, a little shallow, but otherwise she exudes a warm, capable endurance.

The old lady watches her now, as she does often. There is something in her demeanour, perhaps it is her broad chest, which seems to speak of years of care, of love. She imagines new-born babies laid against her shoulder and children bathed by those soft brown hands. She wonders if they, too, will get old, will one day lose their plump firmness, wither and weaken. Will she, too, one day begin the process of forgetting her self, her selves, leaving them behind, faded watercolours in a dusty album?

She turns her attention to the garden. A heart beats through the afternoon. Despite the heat, she can't sleep. She enjoys this time, the time she catches while others sleep. The garden lies bathed in sunlight. Bees hum in half-hearted drones at flowers that nod sagely like monks at prayer. The intermittent coo of a dove sounds, but the air itself is still.

There is a sudden noise from the doorway, the brisk sharpness of shoes tapping down the verandah steps. It is Amelia with the boy. The grass is soft and springy, but she hardly notices for it is the sun that occupies her attention. It beams down directly, a great hot light, and even insects, lizards and birds move restlessly away from it. It is not yet the time for the sprays to be switched on, for the cool tic-tic-tic to remind her that the day is nearing its close. Amelia sighs. She is aware of the time she holds resentfully in her hands. She wants to spill it, to throw it away, but hold it she must and the burden is heavy.

Her son runs at her heels. His small, unstable legs take him rolling across the grass. He cries and she stoops to pick him up. Amelia sighs again and somewhere inside of her, the sigh resounds. She wants to run, to put him down and run, run away. Instead, she feels his skin soft against hers. He is sticky with sweat and his breath is sweet with the sleep he has just woken from. He wriggles and she puts him down, watching him run and fall, run and fall over oceans of grass. Amelia wonders, as she has wondered before, how she would feel if he kept going, through the flowerbed, thick with Julia's daisies and fuchsias, geraniums and petunias; if he crawled through the bougainvillea hedge and carried on into the next garden, and the next, and the next. If he never stopped to look back, if he kept on going and going, his little white legs stumbling, falling, but going ahead, through gardens and flower beds until… then what?

A very slight breeze lifts from somewhere. She shifts her feet and lets the thought detach itself. She hopes it will flutter away, but it drops again, lying heavily next to her. A rustle in the dry leaves makes her start suddenly, but nothing appears.

The old woman and the nurse share a look, a half-smile. There is not a lot of need for them to talk. The nurse is well-versed in the needs of the old. She knows how they squirm under a barrage of talk, she understands how life has become a process of watching and waiting, noticing the little details in life, appreciating quiet. People say how the elderly become like children, but that isn't right. They have a fascination for things in the same way that a child has when seeing something for the first time, but they don't need to touch or examine. They notice what they hadn't seen all their lives long, while other things, like people and words and places, fall away into some empty space behind them.

The old lady, Julia is her name, looks at the garden again. She remembers other days, days pressed firmly like petals in a book. The feeling of grass between toes, the taste of salt on skin, that wonderful exuberance of youth that will never fade, never run out, when life stretches on in an unrolling succession of days without names, without numbers.

She remembers, too, the romance of the young woman cutting white iceberg roses, snipping off withered heads: confident, meticulous, in control, feeling the power of life at her disposal; arranging flowers for a vase, fingers tweaking, lips pursed. She remembers a polished wooden floor, the slant of soft light through a corner window, a child sleeping in a pram, the years that stretched on, ordered and neat. Christmas card lists, holidays to the sea, mending sheets, storing seeds for next year's beds, seasons that folded softly into each other.

There were occasions when she had groaned a little under the weight of time. Times when she wondered just how long it would go on, this making of Christmas puddings and darning of holes. As a child, she loved to climb trees and watch the world from the top of branches. She loved the height and the disguise of leaves and how no-one could find her, although she saw them, the flashes of blue and green of her mother's dress and the white of the cook boy's apron, way beneath her, darting here and there like frightened birds. Sometimes she would imagine she were up there again and she could hide in the thick canopy of green forever.

But the tree was cut down, a long time ago, chopped up for

firewood and, besides, her tree-climbing days were over. And so she had continued to mend socks and wipe children's tears. It was worth it, wasn't it? Those little arms around your neck, the soft kisses, the smiles even while they slept and dreamed it was them climbing trees, climbing and climbing, further and further away into the clouds and beyond.

Forty, Amelia thinks. They had said, hadn't they, that it was too late? You'll be tired. Exhausted. You're not used to children. Having responsibility. The time you need to give up. Your time is not yours. She closes her eyes as she feels time turn elastic. Minutes, hours, all stretched away and away, beyond the garden, beyond all the gardens. Away and away from her, until she is just a small speck, a tiny dot of nothingness. She isn't Amelia, she isn't a mother, she isn't a wife. She is just this tiny spot on a piece of continent, waiting to be whispered away.

Out of the corner of her eye, she sees Julia on the verandah. She knows the old woman's sharp blue eyes are on her. She wonders what she is thinking, of what one can think when one's life is a succession of moves from one room to another, when life has become a routine of waiting, not doing, waiting for an end that must come soon. Life now must surely be whittled down to its basic functions, and even those are not easy.

The nurse gives a little wave and Amelia looks away. She is irritated. Why? The nurse's smile is warm, her face is open. There was an incident. This morning. The boy was crying, his face twisted into ugly red ribbons of childish anger. The breakfast bowl fell from the table and cereal exploded in warm mush on the floor. Amelia picked him up by one arm and took him into the bedroom. He screamed and thumped and lay on the bed, kicking his fat little legs into the air. She turned and closed the door and ignored the pleas to let him out.

She went out onto the verandah, picked up a magazine and flicked through it, seeing nothing but a blur of pictures and tears. Then there was a quiet, a sudden quiet and she realised she couldn't hear the sobs and the sound of the door being repeatedly knocked. She felt a sudden alarm, a tightening of the chest and throat, and dashed along the corridor to his room. The door was open and at once she thought of the goldfish pond and the thick lush green of the water.

Then she heard a voice speaking quietly and the soft shudder of a child's sobs calming into nothing. She saw the nurse carrying him through the garden, talking gently, pointing out flowers and bees and lizards in exaggerated tones of surprise and joy. She saw his little hand grip the nurse's shoulder, his little head nod as she pointed out this and that. His voice still came in hiccups of tears, but he smiled tentatively and the nurse wiped his face.

Julia thinks back down the years, years that flicker and glimmer like a spool of film unravelling. The house had expanded with the laughter of children and dinner parties, friends and visiting family. Her memory jumps from one picture to another: her son receiving a certificate on speech day, her daughters pirouetting through performance after performance and the youngest, another boy, with his Scouts badge. The initial quiet when the children left home was a welcome one. The house sighed with space, but it was never lonely, never empty. She was still the centre, the pivot round which they all swung and to which they all returned. The kisses were less frequent, except when soothing broken hearts, but telephone calls and letters were more insistent.

When she thought they were old enough and she wanted to do something else, something that didn't involve cooking or cleaning or mending, they looked at her as though she had left, as though she stood at the door with her suitcase in hand and kissed them all goodbye. She saw fear in them, the fear of an empty house, as though they couldn't imagine such a life, such emptiness. She stretched out her hands to reassure them it wasn't true, but they didn't believe her, so she folded her dreams away like one of her embroidered cloths and placed them right in the back of the drawer.

Amelia does not want to be here. It isn't her home or her country, but her husband insisted and hung on to his dream of returning home. So clearly had he painted it with the colours of nostalgia that even he was disappointed with the picture he then discovered. He is away all the time; he is getting them a house, he says. Things would be so much better then. If she could just wait, if she could just see what he has tried to tell her all the years they have been together; but even he knows, she thinks. Even he knows, and there is nothing quite so angry, so vicious, as a disappointed soul.

The old lady despises her, she knows that much. She disapproves of the way Amelia dresses and the way she smokes and the way she answers calls on her cellphone, standing outside the house and trying not to let her voice be heard. Be kind, he said, she's very old. She's lonely. Speak to her, please.

172

But Amelia doesn't think Julia is lonely; she is too old to be lonely. Julia mutters to herself and drinks her tea alone and is in bed by eight. There is the nurse who is there all day, humming in the kitchen or singing a few bars of a song or directing the maid where to clean and the gardener where to prune and Amelia can't stand it. She hates the woman's usefulness, her ability to plan and arrange. The nurse made her a cup of tea one day and put it in front of her with a biscuit in the saucer, but Amelia pushed it back ungraciously. I don't drink tea, she said.

At some point, the house had swelled again with grandchildren who fell and tumbled on the soft blanket of lawn or ripped the heads off flowers and plucked the petals out in jest, for such are the actions of the young, who hold life, glimmering and over-brimming, in their hands and then let it spill on the earth at their feet.

Then, gradually, they had started to go. First it was her husband, then friends. People stopped coming to see her; family grew up and moved away. The house contracted. She closed rooms, emptied cupboards, stopped driving. She felt the cold, which seemed to settle in her bones, take up residence with a genial animosity. Her teeth were a problem. Then her leg. And now, the nurse.

Suddenly they were back; her grandson from Australia and his wife and the little one. They clattered and banged doors and left cellphones and car keys on her polished dining table. There were muttered conversations that didn't include her and, from her bedroom, she heard them talking late at night. Sometimes there were the soft sobs of a woman and the sound of doors closing. At times, she wanted to say something, but the woman was hard and unmoving. She wore T-shirts and jeans too tight for her and her mouth was a thin, straight line that smoked cigarettes one after the other. She was always looking somewhere else, out of the window, but not into the garden. Far away, somewhere else, perhaps.

She wonders what will become of the house when she is gone. Her children are scattered throughout the world, not one on African soil. They've all asked her to live with them; they used to plead for her to sell the house and move in with them, but she always shook her head and gave a little laugh. Gradually, they stopped asking. They used to write, letters and postcards. Then just postcards, just Christmas cards. There are occasional phone calls, but sometimes she shakes her head and the nurse tells them she is asleep.

Now, there is her grandson and his awkward little family. She glances at Amelia who watches her little boy collecting leaves with a look of bored abstraction. She wants to tell her she will be all right. Would it help if she put her arm around her? She fears the girl will revolt against her sagging skin and her bony shoulders and her swollen arthritic hands. Everything passes, she wants to say, everything, but Amelia's phone has rung and she picks up the little boy and takes him off to the other side of the garden. The nurse sighs and gives a little shake of her head. She suggests tea and moves off into the house to put the kettle on.

Julia looks up, high into the branches of the syringa. The sun is still bright, still hot, but she feels a shade fall on the house. She leans back in the chair and closes her eyes. She imagines she is a child again and she is climbing, climbing,

climbing. High, high up she goes, right to the top of the great tree. Looking down, she thinks she could perhaps fly if she jumped. She would fly around the house and above the flowers and the top of the hedge. She would fly down the road and then back again. This time, however, she is not interested in flying low. The branches have ended, but she carries on climbing. It becomes colder and lighter and a fine mist comes down and now she is in the clouds. Somewhere, very far away, she hears a teacup placed next to her, the tiny tinkle of a teaspoon placed in the saucer. She hears those hard feet tap up the steps and go inside, but she doesn't mind. She lets go and falls and then swoops and dives.

The garden is hot and silent. The branches of the syringa stretch motionlessly in the sun. Inside the house, it is quiet and dark. The stone floor of the kitchen is cool on bare feet. The little boy wanders from room to room, toddling here and there, looking for the cat that has darted away from his outstretched hands. He disappears into the garden and the house is quiet again. A curtain lifts slightly in a rare breeze and tiny motes of dust dance in a slant of sudden sunlight. The house sighs once more, deeply and slowly, and then it lets her go and she flies.

CHRISTMAS

It's a strange family, ours, a real mixture. I manage to avoid most of them during the year, but not at Christmas. At Christmas they all pop up again for the once-a-year family dinner. Not that we'll all be together this time. For one, Nicholas and Lisa are in New Zealand. They left in March and live in a place called Wellington. I looked it up in my school atlas; it's very far away. They said to me they'd try and come back for Christmas, but Mom says they're really busy and don't have much money, so she didn't expect them home. They sent us a postcard when they first arrived and I wrote back, but I haven't heard from them since, except when they write to Gran.

Gran, now she's a funny one. Eighty-nine this year and still going strong. That's what she always says, even after her hip replacement operation. We had to go to Joburg for that. Mom and Dad and I took her in the car and we stayed at Auntie Lesley's place in Rivonia. We went last school holidays and stayed the whole four weeks. It was fun, except that Mom had an argument with Auntie Lesley because Mom says no one else helps with Gran and we really can't afford it because we live in Zimbabwe. Dad says our dollar is now worth less than the Zambian Kwacha, and we always used to laugh at the Zambians.

Uncle Peter comes from Zambia. He's always talking about it. Dad calls him a 'whenwe' and rolls his eyes every time

176

Uncle Peter says 'when we were in Zambia'. My sister, Linda, says Zimbabweans are like that in England. 'When we were in Zimbabwe' they always say. She lives in London and works in a shop. She does the till. Dad says why leave Zimbabwe to work in a shop, when you can stay here and have a good job? Linda says it's not that easy because you earn more money working in a shop in London than you do in an office in Zimbabwe. Dad shakes his head and says so why are you living in a house with fifteen other people if you're earning so much money? Linda says that's what Zimbabweans do now; they try and help each other out when they first go over and don't have much money. Dad says why don't they help each other out while they're in Zimbabwe, then they wouldn't have to go to England and all squeeze into one house? Linda throws her arms up and shouts, 'Oh I give up!'

Linda worked in Macdonald's for a year. That's how she met her boyfriend, Arnie. He's from Australia and he's a bodyguard. Not much up top though, said Mom after last Christmas when he came back with her. Dad said it was like talking to the dog, except at least the dog responded by wagging its tail or pricking up his ears. When you spoke to Arnie, you could see the words taking a while to sink in. We played Trivial Pursuit after Christmas lunch and he didn't even know which state Brisbane is in. Dad said afterwards that that's like not knowing if Bulawayo was in Matabeleland or not. We even gave him two chances. I'm usually the only one who's allowed two chances, and most of the time Mom holds a book up in front of her face and whispers the answers to me from behind it. I won once, like that. But that's because I'm only ten. Arnie's thirty-two.

At first Mom and Dad were worried about the big age gap between Linda and Arnie, but once they met him, Dad said he felt a whole lot better. He was even too thick to cheat. At one point it was his turn to ask questions, and he didn't even look at the answer first, like Johnnie, that's my cousin, does when he plays. Johnnie's a real cheat, but you have to be quick to be a good one and Arnie's certainly not that. Dad says no wonder the guy's a bodyguard, because if he's shot, even in the head, all they have to do is pick him off the floor, give him a bit of a dust over and he'll be OK again. Probably won't notice anything different.

Typical Aussie, Dad says, but Mom says that's not nice, she's sure there's some really clever ones. Dad says name one and Mom thinks and says, 'Shane Warne.' 'He's a cricket player,' says Dad. 'What's so clever about him?' 'I don't know,' says Mom. 'Anyway, you must be clever to know where to hit the ball so you make the other players run.' 'He's a bowler,' says Dad. 'Oh,' says Mom, 'well, I don't know then.'

Dad went to Australia once on a business trip. Beautiful country, he said. Except for the people who live there, it might be as good as Zimbabwe. Mom said there's a lot of ex-Zimbabweans living there now and Dad got cross and says you're either a Zimbabwean or you're not. You can't be an ex. You can't divorce your country. 'Some people have,' mutters Mom, but he doesn't hear her.

This Christmas, it's going to be quite sad without Pops. He was my Granddad and I know Dad will miss him not being here. Pops died in April. He had a farm out at Nyamandhlovu, not a big place, but big enough for someone to want as theirs. We helped him move all his things into town, but knowing he would never return was too much for him. It wasn't just that. Uncle Chook is buried out there, and Pops loved him so much he felt he was leaving him behind.

Uncle Chook's real name was Charles, but no one ever called him that, except his teachers on his school report. Uncle Chook was only eighteen when he was killed. It was the day after he left Plumtree and came back to work on the farm. He was shot by dissidents, once in the head. We have a picture of him on the dresser. It was taken the week before he died.

Patricia and Glen are also not with us this Christmas; they're in California. Glen's my cousin Johnnie's brother, and he's married to Patricia, a girl he met when he was only sixteen. He's never had another girlfriend. Dad reckons he's a fool not to have played the field a bit before getting hitched, but Mom says it's great; that's what love is, knowing someone is right for you from the start. Dad says every guy should sow his wild oats before he gets married. At first, I thought he meant that every man should be a farmer, but Mom says it's what you say when you think someone should have gone out with a few women before settling down.

I suppose that's what her brother, Uncle Tony, is doing. He's forty-two and he's never been married. He's had lots of girlfriends though, and he's been engaged twice. At the moment he's got a black girlfriend called Delphine. Dad rolled his eyes at first, but now he says she's OK and keeps Uncle Tony under her thumb. It must be quite hard as Uncle Tony is a big guy. He used to play prop for Queens, but now he just props up the bar. Mom's always soft on Tony because he's her little brother. She always sticks up for him, and makes him his favourite meal, steak, egg and chips, when he gets dumped.

She makes it quite often and Dad's told her to go easy on the steak.

The last girlfriend he had, Madeline Oosthuizen, left him for Parkie Monroe. Parkie Monroe's the estate manager at my school. Dad said, 'Now there's one picnic short of a sandwich' when he met Parkie. Imagine him and Arnie as a quiz team, he joked to Mom and I. Parkie's always getting into fights, and he's threatened to beat Uncle Tony up before. Uncle Tony came to my school once to watch Old Boys' cricket and Parkie came up to him near the *boerewors* tent and said, 'Come, come my *boet*, let's settle this once and for all.'

Delphine's bringing her brother to lunch today. We don't know what Dad's going to say because Delphine's brother is a man who likes kissing other men. That's what Mom told me anyway. He's not French (French men kiss each other, but that's OK because that's what they've been trained to do since they were children) but he's gay, which doesn't mean he's happy either. Delphine said she's told him not to wear eyeliner or earrings, so maybe Dad won't guess. Mom says he can't bring his boyfriend this Christmas. Let's do this one step at a time.

I've decorated the tree and the table and made place names for everybody. Dad inspects the seating arrangements and moves the places of those sitting on either side of him. He doesn't want to sit anywhere near Uncle Peter or Gran. 'Are you trying to kill me?' he asks. 'The last thing I need to hear about on Christmas Day is Lusaka, 1969, or Bloemfontein to Esigodeni by ox wagon.'

'That's my mother you're talking about,' shouts Mom from the kitchen. 'Am I ever allowed to forget it?' mutters Dad to me. To Mom, he calls, 'And what a wonderful woman she is!' Mom comes in and hits him with a tea towel. 'You behave,' she says, 'it's Christmas.'

Mom's doing all the cooking and she looks like she needs a break. Dad tells Linda to help, but she's been out all night at some club and she's exhausted. She sits drinking glass after glass of water and won't move when Mom tells her to go and get ready. 'Why do I have to be smart?' she whines. 'It's just family.' 'Hey,' says Dad in a voice that says move your arse or I'll give you a fat crack. 'The Pomms may have lost their standards, but we still have ours.'

Linda's found a new man, a guy from Matsheumhlope, who also lives in London now and they've agreed to meet on Boxing Day. I guess Arnie won't be out here again next Christmas.

Gran arrives first. Well, that's because Dad and I go to fetch her. She lives at Garden Park in a cottage of her own. When we get there, she's already had a few toots with old man de Souza, who lives next door. He's saying, in broken English, that he wants to marry Gran and take her to Lourenço Marques. Dad tells him it's Maputo now, and he's not taking Gran anywhere, she's coming to lunch with us. Gran kisses him goodbye and says, *'Adios amigo.'* Dad says, 'Wrong language, but anyway, get in the car and let's get the hell out of here.'

Then Uncle Peter and Johnnie arrive. They also look like they had a hoolie last night. I know that because Uncle Peter says, 'Just water for me' when Dad asks him what he wants to drink and then Dad does that funny thing with his eyebrows that means 'I give up'. Last year, Johnnie brought his son, Jamie, with him, but this year it's his ex-wife's turn to have him. She's remarried a guy called Pete Parrott. Johnnie says how's that for a name and Dad asks if he's the kind of guy who repeats everything you say. We all laugh. In fact, Mom's cousin, Raymond, used to have a pet parrot that he carried round all day on his shoulder. 'If only I'd known what I was marrying into,' mutters Dad whenever he hears that story.

Uncle Tony arrives with Delphine and Jermaine. Jermaine's not wearing any make up, but he is carrying a handbag and Dad raises his eyebrows when he sees that. He raises them even more when he sees the rings on Jermaine's fingers and Mom coughs and talks loudly before he has time to say anything.

Two hours later, we all sit down for lunch at last. By now the drinks have been flowing and Uncle Tony's got very loud. He excuses himself from the table, but has to hang on to it while he steadies himself a bit. Mom looks at Dad as if to say why did you give him so much to drink? Dad gives her a look as if to say it's not my fault. He goes to use the toilet next door, although Mom's told him before to use the one down the passage so we don't hear him. Uncle Tony always makes a lot of noise when he goes to the loo. Mom tries to talk loudly, but all we can hear is Uncle Tony taking a leak.

'Jeez,' says Dad.

'It's like Vic Falls,' says Uncle Peter.

Uncle Tony doesn't come back into the dining room and I'm sent to find him, in case he's taken the wrong turning and ended up in Mom and Dad's room. It happened once before and, I can tell you, Dad was not impressed. I find him on the phone in the hallway, calling Madeline. He's telling her how much he loves her and what a mistake he made going off with

Delphine. He's forgotten it was Madeline who left him. I go back into the dining room and tell everyone he's coming. It's best not to say what I heard.

Uncle Tony comes back in and Mom starts dishing up. Then his cellphone rings. He can't find it at first, but then he does and he answers it at the table. Mom pulls a face and points outside with her thumb. Uncle Tony ignores her. It's Parkie Monroe. We all know because Uncle Tony starts shouting at him. He ends the call, but it rings again. This time, Delphine answers, much to Tony's horror, and she tells Parkie to stop phoning. Then her face goes black like thunder and she says, 'OK, I'll tell him.' She puts the phone down and turns to Uncle Tony. He's cowering to one side like she's going to hit him with the turkey and she says, 'He says he'll stop phoning *you*, if you stop phoning *her*!'

'Her who?' asks Tony in exactly the same kind of voice I use when Mom asks who's eaten all the chocolates she brought back from South Africa. That's it. Delphine snaps and throws the phone at Uncle Tony. Then she storms out of the room and Uncle Tony runs after her. Jermaine sniggers and rolls his eyes. I can see he's enjoying it. Dad also rolls his eyes, but he's not laughing. 'Only in Bulawayo,' he says.

Mom says to Gran, 'So, how's your new neighbour, Mr de Souza, isn't it?' Dad gives her a look to say 'Don't mention Mr de Souza', but she just looks at him and shrugs. Gran remains tight-lipped. She hasn't forgiven Dad for dragging her away this morning. Uncle Peter starts talking about Zambia and Johnnie helps himself to another drink. Then Delphine and Tony come back in. Delphine looks like she's been crying and Uncle Tony has a large hand mark on one cheek. *Ainar!* That looks like it hurt! But they're OK and that's the main thing, although I had worked out that I might get a considerable amount more Christmas pudding if she, he and Jermaine had left before lunch started.

We're about to start, but just then the phone rings. Dad sighs and throws down his knife and fork. It's for Linda; it's Arnie, phoning with the last credits left on his phone card after phoning his parents in Sydney – that's Sydney, New South Wales, Arnie. He tells Linda he loves her and she comes and tells us he loves her and she loves him. So I expect we'll see Arnie again sometime.

Then Dad raises his glass and says, 'I'd like to make a toast. To absent friends!' Everyone raises their glasses and says 'To absent friends!' and takes a sip of their drinks. I know Dad's thinking about Nicholas and Lisa in New Zealand and Patricia and Glen in California. He's thinking, too, about Pops and Uncle Chook, so long gone now that he no longer cries for him on his birthday. Dad glances briefly at the photo on the dresser, the one of Uncle Chook in his Plumtree uniform, and he tilts his glass slightly in a toast. I know what he's thinking. He's thinking, 'Cheers Chooky! Cheers Pops! Keep me a cold one!' Then he looks away at Mom opposite him and smiles. Mom smiles, too. She's a little tipsy because she doesn't know Johnnie keeps topping up her glass.

'Great meal, love,' he says and puts a forkful in his mouth.

'Hear, hear,' says Uncle Peter and everyone else murmurs 'Hear, hear.' Even Uncle Tony and Delphine and Gran manage a smile so Mom smiles more. Because she's happy. Because it's Christmas. Once again.

MOVING ON

David was standing by the sink, dish cloth in one hand, dinner plate in the other, when Angela said, 'Dad, I want to come with you.' And then, as if to clarify matters, 'To Granddad's funeral. I want to come.'

He hadn't answered immediately, taking time to let the words sink in, pulling in his lips a little, watching his hand making slow circles on the plate with the cloth, as though it were not attached to him at all; as though it were someone else's hand, someone else's life.

She leaned against the kitchen counter, eyeing him with a wary concern. About a year ago, she had decided to shroud herself in black from head to toe, the only bit of colour remaining being the blue of her eyes. The dark eye makeup he found unsettling rather than intimidating, for it suggested a sadness not commensurate with her age and out of kilter with her body, which was young still, thin and angular and inhabited yet by that awkwardness particular to teenagers that, combined with a natural shyness, made her stoop slightly.

In the last year or so, she had become a living ghost, an entity who left the house without saying goodbye and entered it without him knowing. Her bedroom door was always closed, but, unlike other rooms occupied by teenagers from which loud music emitted or from where raucous laughter and insidious giggling slid through the tiny gap between door and carpet, hers was quiet. More than quiet; still. More than once, he had stopped and listened, just for something, anything: a creak of the bed, the soft sound of a pencil being put down on the desk, a cupboard door closing; a sign of life.

A stage, Nancy had said on the only occasion they had ever discussed their daughter's behaviour. It was early one morning in the kitchen and she had been in a hurry putting on her earrings and dialling Marc from the office at the same time. 'It's just girls,' she began. 'Yes, I'll hold. I was like that.' Then she stopped to check herself in the mirror and run a fingertip around her lips to remove any excess lipstick. She pushed back her hair and then fluffed it up at the sides and did that funny shoulder roll that signified she was ready to leave. Then, as though she too were a ghost – or was it him that didn't exist? – she had gone.

'Marc, hi…' She grabbed her handbag and her laptop and made for the door. 'I should be there in five minutes. Listen, I've got some great ideas.'

There was a time when she would have blown a kiss to him and a time before that when she would have planted her lips on his cheek. 'Have a great day,' she would have said, ruffling his hair. 'I'll call you at lunchtime.'

David turned back to his daughter, who had shifted her gaze away from him and was attempting to assume the attitude of bored nonchalance that usually occupied her being. She wasn't quite successful for it was a look edged with a sense of disquiet, of waiting. It was the most impatient he had seen her. Aware of him watching her, she proceeded to channel this restlessness away from herself by taking a sip of water from a long glass then looking down at her nails, which were bitten to the quick and covered in black nail polish. She rolled two thin black plastic bangles up her wrist revealing a small tattoo of a rose, which he had not noticed being there before.

'Yes,' he said, placing the dinner plate on top of another one and reaching for a bundle of knives and forks. 'OK, yes. You can come. But you do know where it is, don't you?'

She put down the glass with a roll of her eyes.

'Africa?' He noticed a tongue stud. That was new too, wasn't it? Or was it? How long was it since they had last talked?

'Zimbabwe.'

She shrugged and nodded her head and then looked away from him. The cockiness had gone, replaced by a look of sad uncertainty. Zimbabwe was his territory, the subject on which no one, not Nancy, not Angela, could trespass. It rarely surfaced in conversation now and, if it did, it only elicited a bored response of silence or the occasional grunt in agreement or disagreement or the stock, automatic refrains of 'Oh dear' and 'That's not good'.

Nancy wouldn't come to the funeral, he knew. There had been no suggestion of it when he told her of the phone call. She had been trying on a new dress in the full-length mirror in their bedroom and the announcement seemed something of an irritation. She had paused in the middle of an action, one hand pressing down the front of the dress, the other on her hip, and gave him a look as though to say he could have chosen a better time and not stolen her moment quite so completely. Then she carried on, one hand moving to her stomach, the other to the small of her back.

'Oh dear. When?'

'Last night. In hospital.'

'How?'

'Heart failure.'

'Yes, well. He has had a couple of scares before, hasn't he?' There was a sense of inevitability in her voice, as though something had come to its natural conclusion and nothing was to be done about it. She leaned forward close to the mirror and tweaked an errant hair in her eyebrow. Then, noticing a wrinkle at the corner of her eye, pulled her face into an odd taut smile that momentarily straightened out any lines.

'Yes,' he said, turning away. Her life, the dress, the occasion on which she would wear it, seemed little to do with him.

Later, as they sat silently eating the bolognaise he had made, he reading his book, she some financial report, she had looked across at him with a twinge of guilt and squeezed his hand. He withdrew his and turned a page.

'I'm going,' he said, without looking up. 'To the funeral.'

'Which is?' The hardness returned to her eyes, which narrowed slightly as she watched him.

'Tuesday.'

'Tuesday? But today is only—'

'Thursday.'

'Yes, Thursday. We're going away for the weekend, remember? We've had it booked for months.'

He paused while he fought the desire to tell her that *she* had had it booked for months and that he didn't want to go anyway, funeral or no funeral. He didn't like her so-called friends who were really just the people from the office; the way they talked business over breakfast and excused themselves to answer what were always urgent phone calls, making out that they didn't want to disturb the conversation but doing just that anyway by pacing up and down, phones in hand, rubbing their foreheads and rocking back on their expensive heels as though the fate of the world depended on them, so that all eyes followed them, waiting for their return and the inevitable words: 'Whew! Close call. If you'll excuse me, I need to do some work before lunch.'

He wanted to tell her that people didn't generally choose when to die. That they don't ask to have a look at diaries and memorise appointments so they can choose a quiet moment whilst no one is doing anything in which to slip away. He wanted to remind her that his father had died and that a little more sympathy may be in order.

Instead he said, 'I've booked the flight. I leave on Saturday.'

Perhaps out of some vague sense of respect or an awareness that she had not quite responded appropriately to his loss, she remained quiet, pushing a small pile of spaghetti to the side of the plate and marooning it there before putting her knife and fork together.

It annoyed him, the way she left the pasta. She had served herself hardly any in the first place as though again what she did take was out of some sense of misguided deference to his loss, but she couldn't carry the action through in its entirety and now heaped it on the side of the plate.

She took a sip of wine. 'I see.' She dabbed the corners of her mouth with a napkin and seemed to be waiting for him to say something. Apologise, maybe, but he didn't.

When the plan to take Angela with him was announced, the last of Nancy's sympathy for him evaporated.

'She won't go,' she retorted.

189

'She was the one who asked.'

Nancy was about to say something, but stopped and drew the words back in, snapping her mouth shut over them.

He obviously wasn't worth arguing with and the next moment she was in Angela's bedroom, the door firmly shut. He stood in the passage, listening hard, and was briefly reminded of the times when Angela was a little girl and how he used to read her to sleep and then creep quietly away, shutting the door behind him and then stopping a moment to listen in case she had woken up.

Those were the days when Nancy didn't work and he went to an office every day. He had treasured those moments with Angela then, sitting on her bed and reading her his favourite childhood classics, watching as her eyes became heavy with sleep and she stuck her thumb in her mouth and cuddled up to her teddy.

It was to Angela that he had first told his Reg Browning tales. Fluent in isiNdebele, Reg was a boy who grew up in the bush in Africa, spending his days hunting and fishing. He was always tanned brown by the sun and knew how to make fire by rubbing two rocks together and how to carve whistles from pieces of wood with a pen knife. Indeed, Reg Browning lived in a timeless age in which politics played no part and there was no war or strife. It was when Angela had grown out of these stories that David had considered putting them to paper and so his first book had been published. Buoyed up by the success of the first adventure and the commission for subsequent novels, he and Nancy had decided that he would stay at home and write and she could resume her career.

He started as the door opened and Nancy emerged, thin-lipped and obviously annoyed. Seeing him, her mouth pulled to one side and she said in a very efficient school teacher fashion, 'Well, I have told her what to expect. Malaria and flies.'

'You don't get malaria in Bulawayo.'

She flicked his comment aside. 'And flies. And she'll have to boil the water no doubt and what's she going to do without electricity – well, that's her problem.' She looked at him down the length of her nose as though to suggest it was his problem as well.

'They do have electricity in Zimbabwe.'

'That's not what you said to me the other day when you were listing all the current woes your father was facing.'

He winced, but stayed calm. 'They might have power cuts but it's not as though they don't ever have electricity.'

Her look this time suggested he better check his facts.

'Look,' he said, wishing he didn't feel he was trying to placate her. 'It's a week, a week and a half at most.'

'A week and a half?'

He paused, looking at a white spot in the carpet halfway between them where, in the phase before the goth phase, Angela had spilt blonde hair dye. It looked like an island in a deep green sea, a tiny island washed by emerald waves. 'I thought I might take her to Victoria Falls.' And then, somewhat superfluously by way of explanation, he added, 'She's never been.'

She stared at him before shaking her head and breathing out noisily.

'So, that's decided then.' She held his glance and then looked away. He walked back into the kitchen and made a list. Somewhere he felt a vague sense of triumph.

David lay in bed at the bed and breakfast in Bulawayo, thinking back on the last time he had seen his dad alive. It was three years ago and he had come to visit them in Brisbane. They had gone fishing on Peel Island and, although they did not catch much that day, what stayed with him was the sense of closeness he had felt to his father. He admired the man: the way he looked like a healthy sixty-five-year-old rather than eighty-three; the way he still managed to get around with ease and how he approached everything in life with a quiet optimism. At his father's core, David realised, was a great strength, a deep something that weathered every crisis. He didn't get annoyed or upset. His inner calmness buoyed him through the storms of life.

It annoyed Nancy, David knew that. Nancy thrived on deadlines and panic. Her day was a frantic emptying of the hourglass; for her, the sands of time seemed to run out more quickly, spurred on by an ever-enveloping feeling that there was never enough. He didn't realise until moments like this how much her frenetic approach to life had rubbed off on him. Like his dad, he stepped back from life, but unlike his dad, he watched it as a scared child might watch large waves come crashing in on the beach: frozen, afraid to run in either direction, hoping against hope that some outside force would bear him up and out of harm's way.

'Are you happy?'

'Yes,' he had said in response to his dad's question, although his reply was just that fraction of a second too slow to be considered an honest one. His dad had tilted his head sideways to look at him and let out his line a little more.

'That's good,' he said with a smile. 'I'm glad.'

David was reminded then of another time in his life when he was a child and he hadn't told the truth. Instead of castigating him, his dad had dropped to his haunches and put a hand on his shoulder.

'When you lie,' he had said, 'the only person you are trying to fool is yourself.'

David turned over in bed. It was a single for he had given the queen-sized bed to Angela. There was something comforting about the simplicity of a single bed. It reminded him of childhood, before life got complicated, before he got entangled in someone else's dreams. It reminded him of a time when, with a teenager's singularity of vision, he focused only on his life's purpose, when he lay on his back and dreamed of all the places he would go to, all the things he would do.

'How long have you lived in Australia?' the lady at the bed and breakfast had asked him as she had struggled to hold a large green and white umbrella and open the front door of the cottage at the same time. They had arrived the previous evening in the middle of a thunderstorm.

'Oh, about twenty years,' he had answered, but now as he lay in bed he realised it was much longer. Thirty-two.

'I hope you don't mind,' the lady had begun as she switched on the lights in the main bedroom, 'we have a dog.' She looked apologetic, as though the decision to keep the animal depended entirely on him. 'He's a lovely dog.' He watched the way she twisted the cottage key in her hands. 'That's yours,' she said, handing it over. 'He's just a bit big and bouncy. Doesn't know his own strength.' She gave a nervous shrug of her shoulders, a gesture that seemed at once an appeal for help and a resignation, as though the matter were entirely beyond her.

And then, in an attempt at jollity: 'So are you here on a holiday?' She looked between him and Angela as though trying to work out the dynamics of the tired, lonely-looking pair.

'No,' he answered. 'My father died. We're here for the funeral.'

'Oh, I'm sorry.' She looked pained and her anxiety over the dog was momentarily forgotten.

'He was in a home,' he said, although he didn't know why for there was no need to explain. 'He was very fit for eighty-six, but he had a fall in the shower last July.'

'Last July?' she repeated, and he knew what she was thinking. It took you all this time to come.

'He was in good hands,' he began. 'He was very well looked after.'

She looked away as though she had delved too deep. 'Well, I'll leave you to it. I am sure you're very tired. Good night.'

Now, as he lay watching a watery sun rise through the torrent of rain that still fell outside, he wondered at the honesty of his words. About a month after receiving the news of his father's accident, he had got an email from Anne, the sister of a friend from Bulawayo, asking him if he knew that his dad was on the most basic of medical aids, which was not covering the smallest of bills. Some of the expenses had been paid by an anonymous well-wisher and others by a donation from a charity for the elderly, but should he need further care, which was inevitable, was it at all possible for David to contribute?

The message had lodged like an arrow through his throat. He felt physical pain when he read the words. Over and over he read them; there was nothing accusatory about them, but he couldn't help feel a vague sense of criticism. He hadn't known; Dad had never said he was in need. Of course, David had bought his ticket when he came to visit and paid for everything while he stayed. But his needs had been minimal beyond the obvious ones of food and a place to stay. He never asked for anything, never seemed to want or need more than he had.

When Angela awoke, he made them tea. She didn't eat breakfast and he wasn't hungry. At eight, he and Angela went to the nursing home to collect his father's paperwork.

'Everything's ready to take,' the matron had pronounced in a bright, bustling manner as she unlocked the door to his room. She stood back to let them in, her eyes scanning Angela suspiciously. 'Take your time. We don't have anybody coming until Friday.'

David stood in the middle of the tiny room that his father had occupied and looked from the single bed pushed alongside one wall to the table in a corner on which stood a small bottle of Mazoe Orange, a glass and three old *Angler's Mail* magazines. On a shelf above the table was a photo of David's mother when she was in her early forties and one of David and Nancy with a very small Angela.

'Is this it?' Angela asked, looking around too. 'It's more like a jail cell.' Their eyes met and she looked away. 'Sorry,' she added, 'It's just... I'm sure it's very nice here.'

His dad's clothes were laid out on the bed and his drawers emptied. David ran his hand along the collar of a blue shirt, one of two, trying not to notice how the material was frayed and worn. He smoothed a crease out of a pair of trousers and then let his hand fall limp beside him.

'Look, Dad,' said Angela, who had pulled a child's painting from behind the family photo. It was one that she had painted at pre-school many years ago after one of her grandfather's visits. 'I remember doing this. He had just left and I missed him.' She held up the now-faded picture of a stick man with a large head and glasses and a large smile that took up most of his face. 'He kept this. All these years.'

David declined the matron's offer of a cup of tea, instead asking where his father's personal papers were.

'Oh, the undertaker's got those,' she stated, nodding her head.

'The undertaker? You mean the funeral has been arranged already?'

'Oh yes,' she nodded again. 'It's the standard one we offer here. Service in the chapel followed by tea in the lounge.'

'And will he be buried or cremated?' David felt a hot flame of anger dart up his throat. He swallowed hard and took a deep breath.

'We're very lucky to have a plot allocated to us in the cemetery. Our board worked very hard to be given it.' She leaned forward in a conspiratorial manner. 'You don't want to be buried just *anywhere* in Bulawayo.' Another nod of the head.

'My father...' David began, then, feeling his throat contract, he stopped. 'My father always wanted to be cremated.'

'Well, unfortunately, the crematorium isn't working at the moment.' She raised her eyebrows meaningfully. 'But, luckily, we have this plot—'

'Yes,' David interrupted her. 'You said.'

That night after the funeral, Anne asked them to dinner. He
had been a school friend of her brother, Peter, who now lived
in Canada. Her eyes flickered over Angela in surprise, but she
said nothing. David had warned his daughter that
Zimbabwean society was still quite conventional and that they
had probably no idea of goths in Bulawayo. Yet Anne's
teenage son and daughter looked upon Angela with interest
and immediately tried to engage her in conversation. Not
immediately forthcoming in response, Angela had refused a
glass of wine and opted for water instead. She pushed a small
helping of chicken casserole round her plate, taking small,
wary nibbles when she felt the need to show she was eating
something.

The evening was a little stiff at first, especially after the first
perfunctory remarks about politics and weather and who was
doing what and where. Afraid of being drawn into the
problems of everyday life in Zimbabwe, David had trod
carefully on the edges of the conversation. They spoke about
Brisbane and Australia and his writing.

'Your books do quite well, don't they?' Anne asked.

'Yes,' he answered. 'Apparently so.'

'I read a write-up once in a South African magazine.'

'Yes.' He tried to think of an appropriate rejoinder but
words seemed to have escaped him.

Anne ate quietly, staring at her plate.

'So where do you get your ideas from?' she asked. 'It must
take a lot of working out.'

David's heart sank. It was the stock question of
inexperienced interviewers.

'Oh, here and there.'

She nodded. 'Quite amazing really.'

He looked sideways at her, not understanding the meaning of her remark.

'What I mean is, writing about Africa in the way you do and yet you haven't been here for years.'

The look he gave her this time was sharp and alert. He detected a prod behind the words, a hard dig.

'When, in fact, was the last time you were here?'

In the end, it was a relief when the coffee had been drunk and David could excuse them without rudeness.

The day after the funeral, David woke early. The rain had stopped and the day was brightening into a slow grey. He carried his running shoes to the door quietly and had a quick look into Angela's room. She lay sprawled on the bed, still clad in black, like a long thin spider. Her face was surprisingly clear of makeup though, her lips a natural pale pink. From this angle, she looked like Nancy, a much younger, relaxed Nancy, and David felt a momentary twinge, not for her, but for a time that seemed irrevocably gone. He pulled the family picture from his pocket and stared at it a full minute before putting it away.

He closed the front door behind him gently and walked down the long drive to the gate. As quiet as he thought he had been, the dog must have heard him and bounded closely behind him. It jumped up at him, landing its huge paws on his shoulders. He pushed it down and stroked its head, which it twisted upwards in a playful attempt to bite his hand. He unlocked the gate, opening it just enough to squeeze himself out. The dog pawed at the gate, but he managed to close it behind him.

'Good dog,' he said. 'Good dog.'

The dog whined and wagged its tail, waiting to be let out, but David ignored it and turned right onto the road. It was littered with potholes that had filled with rainwater and the verges were thick with long green grass that was nearly as tall as he was. A lamppost leaned dangerously close to the ground. A couple of cars splashed through puddles or swerved recklessly to avoid them. A few people walked along: a schoolgirl holding her mother's hand, a maid in uniform, a man pushing a bike.

At the next junction, the road signs were missing, but he thought he knew where he was. The roadside was overgrown and the road itself dilapidated, but not much else had changed in the last thirty or so years. If he was right, their house was at the bottom of the road on the left.

On the back cover of each of his books was a short biography of David March. It read: 'Growing up in Rhodesia (now Zimbabwe), he spent his boyhood in the bush where he developed a love and knowledge of the outdoors.' In reality, he had grown up in town, in the leafy suburb of Hillside, but his publicist had insisted on changing the details to suit the readership. In fact, one interviewer had gone so far as to suggest he had grown up in a mud hut without electricity or running water and, although David had felt the lie had gone too far that time, it had almost certainly upped the sales of *Running Brave*, the third book in the series.

He stood outside the house; this was it. It must be. The basic wrought-iron gate had been replaced by a huge black electric monstrosity and the hedge by a wall above which a bougainvillea stretched like a long pink feather boa. Unsure, he looked at the house next to it, which still had a fence through which he could see the garden and part of the house. He considered ringing the bell, but it was still early and he didn't want to wake anyone. Besides, he didn't want to have to explain. I used to live here. About twenty, no thirty, years ago. Australia. No, not a holiday. My father died. He was in a home.

He looked away. In the pocket of his shirt, he could feel the photograph rub against him.

Are you happy? Are you happy? He lives in Brisbane with his wife and daughter and their funny cat, Max. Are you happy? They enjoy taking walks together as a family and spending their weekends exploring south-east Queensland. You can lie to everyone, but you can't lie to yourself.

Are you happy?

Suddenly, David ran at the wall and tried to jump, but he fell back. He tried again, taking a longer run up this time, but again he failed. The third time, he stared hard at the wall before running with all his might, hands up, reaching, clawing for the top of the wall, which was rough and hard and cut his fingers. He leapt back in pain and lay sprawled on the wet grass, holding his hurt hand, squeezing back the tears.

'Dad? What on earth are you doing?'

It was Angela. In black, she was always in black. Always mourning – what? She looked as though she had been crying for streaks of black smudged across her face. Couldn't she go for a walk without metamorphosing beforehand?

'I'm just… going for a walk.'

'Looks like it,' she said, pulling him up.

He sat up, embarrassed that a tear had managed to escape, but she turned a blind eye.

'I was just looking for our house. We used to live – here, I think. Except we didn't have a wall or an electric gate.'

She looked up at the wall without much interest.

'How would anyone know what's behind that. You could have lived in any of these houses. They all look the same.'

'No they don't, Angela,' he snapped. 'They don't look the same!' It was the first time he had lost his temper with her for years. 'It's obvious,' he said, motioning to the wall with his outstretched hand, which was bleeding slightly. 'It's obvious that this house here is different to that house *there*.'

'Dad! You don't have to get so... so angry.'

'Don't I? Don't I?' He grabbed her by the shoulders and pushed her towards the wall of the garden. 'This was my house, this was my childhood, this is where *I grew up*.'

She looked wildly, blindly at the wall, pulling her shoulders together as though she were cold.

'Look, look! What do you see? Come on, tell me. *What do you see?*' He was shouting loudly now. A man and a woman stopped to look, then catching his eye, they walked on. He turned her round and round, his fingers digging into her shoulders, hurting her back.

She started to cry. 'I don't know, Dad. I don't know. I don't know what you want me to see.'

His hands dropped by his sides in exasperation and he was just about to launch another attack when a large dog bounded up and knocked him to the ground.

'You didn't close the gate,' he said, accusingly. He wiped a spot of blood off his forehead and rubbed his hand. 'You let the dog out.'

'I am sorry,' she said. 'I didn't mean to. I thought the gate was closed.'

He stood up and made a grab for the dog's collar, but it

swerved its head and sprang back, ready to play. He made another move to catch hold of it, but the dog was off, chasing a smell in the grass.

'Get it! Catch him!' shouted David, and Angela, who was hugging her shoulders together, jerked forward in a halting, staccato manner, but the dog evaded her too and bounded onto the road where it looked back, tongue hanging out, waiting.

'Bloody dog! Bloody dog!' shouted David, his hand smarting in pain from where he had torn it on top of the wall.

'Come here, come here,' Angela called to it softly. 'Good boy, come on.'

But the dog turned on his heel and trotted off down the road, stopping to snuffle in a drain, before disappearing into some long grass.

'What the hell are we going to do now?' exclaimed David. Angela didn't answer, biting her lip and shying away from his anger.

'I'll get him.' Her lip trembled. 'I'll get him. It's my fault.'

'It's not your fault. I didn't mean…'

'No, Dad. It's true. I should have been more careful. I'm sorry, I'll get him.'

'I'm the one who's sorry. I don't know what happened.'

'Dad, stop it. Please, just stop it. You always do this.'

'Do what?'

'Apologise. I hate it. If you mean something, say it. Just *say* it. Don't say it and then say you didn't say it.'

'I'm sorry.'

She rolled her eyes, which were glistening with tears. '*Dad!* This is not one of your books. You can't go back and edit; you can't take back what has been said. You're not in control of the beginning and the end and the next chapter and who says what and why.'

'I...' he stopped and slumped against the wall. The hard granite dug into his back. He squeezed his hand. He wanted to feel pain, sharp pain, course through his body.

'Oh, Angela...' he began but the pain was too much. It ran wildly through his body, swamping it with an unbearable agony, a torment of both physical suffering and overwhelming grief. At first, he tried to hold it back, to keep it in its place, but the torrent was too strong and fast and there was a relief, too, a peace, in letting go.

He cried in great racking sobs, letting his body double up under the weight of its sorrow. He let the tears come. Let his arms collapse limply next to him, let his head roll to the side. He felt arms around him and a face next to his.

'Angela,' he said. 'Angela...'

'I know, Dad,' she said, holding him close. 'I know.'

Early in the morning four days later, the lights of a taxi turned into the drive of the bed and breakfast and stopped outside the cottage.

'Taxi's here, Dad,' said Angela, putting down her mug of tea.

He looked across at her and nodded. It was unusual to see her dressed in something other than black. She had bought a brightly coloured T-shirt at Victoria Falls and red, green and gold wire earrings. He was surprised at how much more mature she suddenly looked and realised with a pang that she was nearly grown up.

'Mum messaged,' he said, looking down at his phone.

'Good,' she replied, not looking at him.

'She's looking forward to seeing us again.'

Angela nodded and stood up, scooping up the pile of passports and tickets.

They closed the door to the cottage and let the taxi driver place their two suitcases in the back of the taxi.

'Time to go, Dad,' said Angela, as the car moved down the road. She squeezed his arm.

David looked down at his phone and considered sending a reply to Nancy's message.

'Just leaving,' he tapped out. Then he stopped, his forefinger hovering over the keypad before adding: 'See you soon.'

WHATEVER HAPPENED TO RICK ASTLEY?

She placed the lasagne in the oven, closed the door and hung the oven gloves on a hook on the wall. Forty-five minutes. Then it would be ready. She often marvelled at how what went in the oven was so different to what came out; how it all bubbled and melted and congealed into something else, something deliciously palatable.

Her grandmother had once made an analogy between a stew and a marriage. It was very important to put in all the right ingredients, yet they alone could not guarantee the success of the meal. The right oven is crucial: temperature, position and time. It was important not to rush anything, not to open the oven before time, not to poke and prod and turn the heat up to rush things on. She poured hot water onto a peppermint teabag in a mug, picked up her phone and went to await the return of her family on the comfort of the couch.

She had made lasagne so many times, it was always perfect. It was their Friday night meal, the sign that the weekend had arrived. Victor would come home from work via the sports club bar where he would have had a beer or two and a game of darts. Even though Scott was working and spent most evenings out with friends, she knew he would be looking forward to his lasagne when he got home, however late that might be. It still made her happy to be making his favourite meal, even if the little boy's wide-eyed delight had been replaced by a cursory nod of his head as she placed a plate of food in front of him.

She didn't mind. Nor did she mind the mess he made: the dirty plate left on the sofa, the glass on the floor, the empty dish on the table surrounded by flecks of tomato sauce. She had minded more when he was younger, when his time at home was eternal, but now he was a young man, she dreaded the time he would move out.

It seemed like just the other day that she had held him as a baby; just the other day that she had lain awake at night, rubbing her swollen belly, contemplating the years that lay before them both. Before that – a young, houseproud wife saving for a new kettle, a new iron, a new set of mugs. And before that, too, the bride in white, the girl engaged, secretarial college, school. The pages of memory flicked past; years compressed into smiles and poses: birthdays and Christmases, picnics and outings, holidays and celebrations.

How is it, she thought, that time can pass so endlessly slowly from the window of a classroom? How can it lie looped and coiled in great piles of delicious life with all its promise of choice and possibility, and yet, without you noticing, unwind so fast? She saw it suddenly – how change was always there, surreptitiously working its way through life – the haircuts, the length of skirts, the archness of a smile. It caught you unawares. Yet it was the future that she feared: all those blank pages.

In a bid to brighten her thoughts, she picked up her phone and flicked to Facebook. There were the usual comments. *Wonderful day out with friends.* She clicked 'love'. *Feeling so good in my new dress.* She clicked 'like'. *Friday special on beef.*

'Like'. *Look who's wearing Daddy's shoes.* That deserved a 'ha ha'. And there was a sad face for *Pranged my car as I drove out the parking area today. Tim not very happy with me.*

She carried on scrolling down through the sea of grinning faces, smiling groups of people with raised glasses, cute pets, children, quotes, adverts, pictures of exotic destinations, beautiful birds, wild animals at dusk.

Someone had posted a video. *The good old days* they said. She pressed play. It was Rick Astley. Rick Astley in his dark suit, hair quiffed. Rick Astley walking down the stairs, young and suave. It brought back memories of those years just after she had left school. She still lived at home, but she and Victor were dating. One memory in particular stood out and it made her smile to remember it.

She was in her bedroom with the music playing loudly while she tried on outfit after outfit. Dresses and jackets and trousers and skirts. Then there was the make up: the lip gloss and the blush and the thick mascara. *Never gonna...* The big hoop earrings and the arm full of bangles in different colours... *give you up*. She was going to a concert; that was what she told herself. She and Vic had front row seats to see Rick Astley. She closed her eyes and waved her arms in the air.

Rick, Rick. Over here, Rick. She could feel the throng behind her as people fought their way to the front. She felt herself surge forward and thought she was going to stumble, but there was Vic, his hand on her hip, and he pulled her closer to him. That smell of cologne, of aftershave, of a man. And suddenly her dad was shouting from the kitchen had anyone seen the scissors and she lowered her arms and looked at herself in her dressing table mirror.

There was no concert, but she could imagine, couldn't she? She picked up a luminous pink top and held it against herself as she twirled in front of the mirror. *I've been meaning to tell you...* She turned to the poster of Rick Astley on the wall above her bed, singing along to the music as though she were singing to him. Rick in his polo neck, his baby face smiling, his eyes on her.

She felt a gentle but sudden lurch in her stomach. Rick Astley with his whole life ahead of him. Her hand went out to touch the screen, but then she stopped. She was quite suddenly and overwhelmingly aware of a silence in the house. It began to stretch and balloon and she in turn began to feel a certain distress. It was not an enjoyable silence for there was an emptiness to it, a feeling like dusk, of the end of things, of the impending darkness, the narrowing of night. She took a sip of her peppermint tea and pressed play again on the YouTube video.

But she couldn't get the feeling back, however much she tried to imagine her bedroom with all the posters and her overcrowded dressing table with all her necklaces and bangles and earrings and scarves. All the time, she was in the present in the house, feeling the quiet tug at her sleeve.

Whatever happened to Rick Astley? She imagined that he was happily married with children. A record producer, perhaps? That was the usual way with singers, wasn't it?

In her mind's eye, she saw him in a room in a large house. The room was a studio with all sorts of recording equipment and chrome chairs. There were black and white pictures on the wall of Rick, hair back, looking thoughtful, staring into the distance, hand on chin, quietly contemplative, alluringly distant. All pictures of his younger self that he trailed behind him like a little boy holding his kite to the wind, watching it soar way above him, giggling delightedly. Rick helping other people become successful. He was the mature voice of knowledge and insight. He knew the way things were done.

In other rooms, children played or did their homework at desks. His wife, home from work, organised dinner. A lasagne. Except it wasn't homemade. It was in a large foil takeaway container. She put it in the oven and set the timer. Then she made a salad and set the table. Opened a bottle of white wine and poured herself a glass.

A sound brought her out of her reverie. She thought it was that of the back door closing and got up to see if Victor was home. The kitchen was empty.

'Hello?' she called, expecting to see her son pulling the oven door ajar to see if supper was ready, but there was no one there. All was quiet except for the steady tick of the oven timer. She looked around at the table laid neatly with place mats and cutlery, the chairs pushed in, the clean surfaces of the counter, the sink empty of dishes and plates for she had washed everything and put it away.

For a few seconds, the room seemed to darken with a deep red light, as though she was looking through a red filter. She felt a deep loss: they had all gone, they didn't need her anymore.

She had never known, never even guessed that this was how her own mother must have felt as she and Victor, that night after the movies, had sat at the table, in front of the food her mother had insisted they eat and, after exchanging shy giggles and knowing looks, had told her the news. We are getting married.

What had she missed? She found herself scrabbling through memories. Her mother congratulating her and Victor. Her father shaking Victor's hand. Her mother and her planning the wedding dress, looking through the kist for her grandmother's tiara, showing her the linen and household items that she saved for every month.

There was one memory. Some weeks before she got married, she had come home late one night and missed dinner. Her mother sat at the kitchen table in her blue dressing gown, sipping a cup of tea. The table was set for one. There was a plate of food covered with a cloth and an empty glass with a jug of water next to it.

'Mom,' she exclaimed, surprised. 'Why did you wait up? It's late.'

'You haven't eaten,' said her mother, moving to get a dish out of the warmer. 'There's salad on your plate. The rest is in here.'

'Oh, I'm not hungry. I've eaten.'

'Did you? What did you have?'

'We had a burger and then we had a big ice cream,' she said, slinging her bag on the back of the chair. 'And coffee. I'm exhausted.' She sat down, her head on her hands.

'A burger's nothing. I have made spaghetti bolognese. Let me get you some.' Her mother picked up the oven gloves.

'No, no. I'm off to bed.'

'Are you?' She couldn't quite hide the note of disappointment in her voice. 'But it's your favourite.'

She smiled. 'Mom, I'm tired. You must be tired.'

'I'm all right.'

'Just think – a couple more weeks and I'll be out of here.'

'I don't think like that.'

'Forever!'

'It's not a problem. I like cooking.'

'You won't have to wait up for me ever again. You can go to bed!'

She stood up to go to her room, yawning widely.

'You go and sleep,' said her mother. 'I'll just tidy up in here.'

That's what she had done, wasn't it? She had gone to bed. But not before she had turned back just for a moment – and what had she seen? A sudden flicker of an old woman, slightly stooped, stirring the contents of a dish. She had wanted just then to throw her arms around her mother's neck and hold on to her, but she hadn't.

It was long ago, but yesterday, too. *Together forever...*

She caught sight of herself then in the mirror near the front door. Fifty-two, dark hair streaked a little grey. Slightly overweight. Cuddly, Victor would have said, but he no longer did.

'Hello,' she said again, but this time it was not a question.

She leaned in a little closer, tracing the lines on her forehead and under her eyes. Then she stood back and pulled her stomach in, staring at her profile, holding her breath until she couldn't anymore. She rummaged in her handbag for a lipstick and applied two or three coats. She also found a small free perfume tester she had been given and dabbed it on her wrists. Then she gave her hair a good brush and tied it up in a high ponytail.

'Whatever happened to you?' she said aloud to the mirror. 'Whatever happened to me?'

'Whatever happened to Rick Astley?' she said as she passed the salad down the table to Victor.

'Who?' mumbled Victor through mouthfuls of lasagne.

'Rick Astley. You know – *Together forever and never to part.*'

Victor turned his nose up. 'Was he that guy who wandered around in a long black coat with a red rose looking permanently constipated?'

She laughed. 'That was Michael Bolton. Rick Astley was… well, Rick Astley. I just wonder what happened to him.'

'Dead, probably.'

'Dead? He's not dead. He can't be. Not Rick Astley. He wasn't one of those druggy types.'

'Who wasn't one of those druggy types?' said Scott, who had come home without their knowledge.

'Rick Astley.'

'Mmm, lasagne. I'm starving,' said Scott.

'Sit, sit. I'll get it for you.'

'OK, but quick. I want to watch something that may already have started.'

She dished up for him and he loped off to eat in front of the television.

'I just wonder what happened to Rick,' she said, easing back into her chair. 'I haven't thought of him in years, but today—'

'Oh, for God's sake!' exclaimed Victor. 'Who the hell cares? I tell you, the guy's dead.'

There was a silence. Embarrassed, Victor added: 'Either that or he's a second-hand car salesman.'

'No, he's not.' She began to collect the plates. For some ridiculous reason, she wanted to cry. 'He wouldn't be. He was a talented guy.'

Victor got up and joined Scott in front of the television. She started to wash the dishes. Even if someone had offered to help, which they didn't, she wouldn't have taken it. There was something both soothing and rewarding about doing the washing up.

A while seemed to pass. She put the dried plates and cutlery away and wiped the kitchen counters.

'Never gonna give you up,' she half sang, half hummed. 'Never gonna let you go…'

'Down,' said Scott, coming up behind her and making her jump.

'What?'

'Never gonna let you down. Not go.'

'Oh, I never did get lyrics right.'

'He's back, you know? He's released a few new albums since you were young.'

'Young*er*, thank you very much. So he's not a second-hand car salesman?'

'And he's not dead. You should listen to some of his new stuff. I'll download it for you.'

She smiled but shook her head. 'I think I'd like to leave him as he was.'

'Weird,' he said. 'But the choice is yours.' He turned to go and then turned back. 'You look nice, Mom. You should do your hair like that more often.'

She put her arms round him in a sudden hug, squeezing him hard. When she stood back, her eyes were glistening with tears.

'Mom?'

'Go on, get out of here,' she said, waving his embarrassment away with a tea towel. 'Leave me to my kitchen and my memories.'

Later that night in bed, unable to sleep, she picked up her phone and searched Google for Rick Astley.

Rick Astley retired from the music industry in 1993 to bring up his daughter. However, he returned in 2000 to release his new album. His daughter now lives in Denmark.

The words brought a strange sense of peace. Somewhere between the past and the present, he had returned and she hadn't noticed. She looked through the titles of his new albums and didn't recognise one, but it didn't matter. She didn't want to. Not because she wasn't interested, but because she wanted to keep him as she knew him. He looked older. Of course he did. Who doesn't? *Older, wiser, but the same old Rick Astley we all know and love.* That's what the review said.

It's all right, she thought as she shared a video of him to Facebook. Rick Astley – he's OK. He did the right thing. His daughter will visit every year from Denmark with her family. There will be Christmases and birthdays. It doesn't have to end. She thought of her mother in her blue dressing gown waiting up for her every Friday and Saturday night. It was about taking the baton and running with it as far and as steadily as possible, and being willing to hand that baton over to the next person, not to hold onto it grudgingly, not to want to run their race for them.

Whatever happened to Rick Astley? she wrote on her post. Then she smiled and added: *He's happy. He grew up.*

ACKNOWLEDGEMENTS

Some of the stories in this collection were previously published. My thanks go to those anthologies.

'The Queue': *Short Writings from Bulawayo*
(amaBooks, 2003)

'The Rhythm of Life': *Short Writings from Bulawayo III*
(amaBooks, 2006)

'Christmas': *Laughing Now* (Weaver Press, 2006)

'The Big Trip': *Women Writing Zimbabwe*
(Weaver Press, 2007)

'The Piano Tuner': *Where to Now?*
(amaBooks, 2011; Parthian Books, 2012)

'Music From a Farther Room': *The Gongon Pin and Other Stories* (New Internationalist, 2014)

'Moving On': *Moving On and Other Stories*
(amaBooks, 2017; Parthian Books, 2019)

'The Fountain of Lethe': *Hotel Africa*
(New Internationalist, 2020)

PARTHIAN Short Stories

Figurehead
CARLY HOLMES
ISBN 978-1-912681-77-8
£10.00 • Paperback

'Through beautiful, rhythmic prose
Figurehead weaves a sequence of stories
that are strange, captivating, and
unforgettable.' – Wales Arts Review

Love and Other Possibilities
LEWIS DAVIES
ISBN 978-1-906998-08-0
£6.99 • Paperback
'Davies's prose is simple and effortless, the
kind of writing that wins competitions.'
– *The Independent*

Local Fires
JOSHUA JONES
ISBN 978-1-913640-59-0
£10.00 • Paperback

'In this stunning series of interconnected
tales, fires both literal and metaphorical
blaze together to herald the emergence of a
singular new Welsh literary voice.'

Grace, Tamar and
Laszlo the Beautiful
DEBORAH KAY DAVIES
ISBN 978-1-912109-43-2
£8.99 • Paperback
Winner of the Wales Book of the Year